Last Breath

A Gideon Johann Western
Book 5

By
Duane Boehm

Last Breath: A Gideon Johann Western Book 5

Copyright 2016 Duane Boehm

For more information or permission contact:
boehmduane@gmail.com

This book is a work of fiction. References to real people, events, establishments, organizations, or locales are intended only to provide a sense of authenticity and are used fictitiously. All other characters, and all incidents and dialogue are drawn from the author's imagination and not to be construed as real.

ISBN: 1-53325-305-6

Other Books by Duane Boehm

In Just One Moment
Last Stand: A Gideon Johann Western Book 1
Last Chance: A Gideon Johann Western Book 2
Last Hope: A Gideon Johann Western Book 3
Last Ride: A Gideon Johann Western Book 4
Wanted: A Collection of Western Stories (7 authors)

Dedicated with love to Sophie – the little girl that changed my world

Chapter 1

The lunch crowd had packed the Last Stand Last Chance Saloon with cowboys, storeowners, and townsfolk. The first sunshine after a couple days of cloudy skies had put the patrons in a jovial mood, forcing everyone to use their outdoor voices in order to carry on a conversation. Sheriff Gideon Johann sat at his usual table with Deputy Finnegan Ford, Doc Abram, and saloon owner Mary Ford. They too were in a fine mood and laughing at another of Finnie's infamous stories.

Mary looked around the room as her employees hustled to keep up with the demand for food. She hated not helping, but she was pregnant and had been forced to put up an epic battle to keep Doc from insisting that she go on complete bedrest. Her previous pregnancy had ended in a miscarriage that nearly claimed her life. She had made it well past the point of her previous miscarriage, but her husband and friends danced on pins and needles concerning her health.

A rancher by the name of Carter Mason walked into the saloon and scanned the crowd until he caught sight of the sheriff. Gideon watched as other patrons scurrying about the saloon interrupted Carter's long strides towards the table. Carter was an affable enough fellow and Gideon admired the way the rancher waxed his mustache into handlebars.

"What brings you to town, Carter?" Gideon asked as the rancher made his way to the table.

Carter had a habit of playing with his mustache as he talked and he started twisting one end of it before he spoke. "I wanted to let you know about something. That sheepherder, Colin Young, his sheep drifted onto my property the other day. I can tolerate sharing free range with those sheep even if I don't like it, but I don't appreciate them grazing on my land. Me and the boys, we drove them off my place. Colin was nowhere to be found. Anyways, I went looking for him at his camp afterwards and couldn't find him. His place looked empty. I thought it odd, but didn't think a whole lot about it. Well, his sheep were back on my place this morning and I rode back over to his camp and he's still gone, but I smelled something dead. It smelled pretty rank. I didn't stick around to find the source of the odor, but I thought that you might want to go take a look," he said.

Colin Young lived in a one-room cave that he had dug out of the side of a bluff. People considered him a hermit and a bit of an eccentric, but he had managed to coexist with the ranchers without ever coming to blows. Nearing sixty years old, rumors persisted that Colin had accumulated wealth and possessed a hidden stash of gold coins buried in the cave.

"Finnie and I will ride out there and have a look. Thank you for taking the time to come to town," Gideon said.

"I just hope that you don't find what I fear you will. Sheep or not, Colin didn't bother nobody," Carter said before leaving.

"Colin stopped in here just a few days ago. He always came in and had one beer whenever he came to town. He'd sit by himself, and if somebody talked to him, then he'd talk, but he'd never start a conversation. I always kind of admired him," Mary remarked.

Looking at Finnie, Gideon said, "I guess we better get out there and see what's going on. I knew we were having too much fun for our own good."

In his thick Irish accent, Finnie said, "Aye, lawmen and fun go together about as well as spinsters and whorehouses."

Mary rolled her eyes at her husband. "How many different sayings can one man have that work whorehouse into the conversation?" she asked.

"Are you sure you're feeling okay? You seem a little irritable to me. I don't want to leave and find out otherwise," Finnie said only half in jest.

"Doc is here with me. The only thing that riles the baby is listening to you fret over us. We both could use a break from you," Mary said and winked at Finnie to soften the blow.

"What are you smiling at, you old sawbones?" Finnie said to Doc. "I suppose you find this all amusing."

"I plead the fifth, but I promise to look after your wife," Doc said.

"Gideon, let's get out of here. I feel about as wanted as the French Pox in a whore – oh, never mind," Finnie said as he shoved his hat down onto his head and stood.

Mary arose from her seat, pushed Finnie's hat off his forehead, and kissed her shorter husband there. "You two be careful out there. Doc and I would be bored out of our minds if we didn't have you to rile all up," she said.

Gideon walked to the jail to get the rifles and his horse while Finnie headed to the livery stable to retrieve and saddle his gelding. By the time the deputy walked his horse out of the stable, Gideon rode up and handed him his rifle. The two men headed southwest out of town. Mountains loomed before them and they followed the trail that snaked through a pass around the first range until they reached the grazing land between the peaks.

"How well do you know this Colin Young?" Finnie asked.

"I remember him from when I was a kid. He always kept to himself and never bothered anybody. The ranchers never took to him because of the sheep, but none of them gave him trouble that I ever heard tell. I've talked to him once since I moved back to Last Stand. He wasn't crazy or anything. He just liked to be alone," Gideon answered.

Gideon had returned to Last Stand three years ago after an eighteen-year absence that began when he left to fight in the war. He had accidently killed a small boy after a skirmish with Confederates and had spent years running from his conscience until returning to town and coming to terms with his past life. Since his reappearance, he had married Abby, his childhood sweetheart, and had a son. He had also been confronted with the shocking news that he had a grown daughter named Joann.

"I don't have a good feeling about this. Hermits aren't known for going off and exploring or leaving their sheep. Especially an old one that's been around forever," Finnie said.

"Well, we're about to find out," Gideon said.

"I've been thinking about something. Now I know that I'm a couple of years younger than you, but did you realize that you're going to become a grandpa a month or so before I become a daddy for the first time," Finnie said. He smiled as he looked over at Gideon and watched his friend sit up straight in the saddle and pull his shoulders back.

"Really? You've already annoyed Mary and now you're going for me. I was only eighteen when Joann was born and I have a son that's not even two yet. It's not like I've been put out to pasture. I'd say it's more a reflection on your late start in life. Some of us figure out how things work a little sooner than others. And I swear that if you ever call me grandpa I'll shoot you on the spot. I don't care if you saved my life or not. Somethings just can't be tolerated," Gideon said.

Finnie let out a giggle and popped his thigh with the flat of his hand. "I guess I've hit a sore spot. Kind of like a burr under the saddle. You're getting to be a sensitive man in the autumn of your life. Maybe I'll just call you Papa," he said.

Colin Young's camp sat over the next ridge and Gideon decided to ignore Finnie's jibes. Otherwise, he would only be giving the little Irishman what he wanted and the needling would never end. It wasn't as if he could really shoot Finnie and there certainly was no way that he could whip him. Gideon had known Finnie since back in the days when they fought side by side in the war and he'd never seen the Irishman lose a fight.

Topping the ridge, the camp looked deserted as they rode down towards the sheepherder's home. The two lawmen caught the scent of something dead that Carter Mason had told them about before they reached the camp. As they walked about, they couldn't find any fresh tracks since the wind had blown hard the previous day. A campfire inside the cave appeared to have burned out days ago and was now reduced to an ash pile. In the middle of the room, an old wooden chair lay turned over and Gideon thought that he could make out three or four different boot tracks around the seat, but he couldn't say for sure.

As they walked out of the cave, Gideon said, "Which way do you think that smell is coming from?"

"Do I look like coonhound to you? This holler makes it hard to tell which way the wind is blowing with the way that it swirls down here," Finnie said.

"Let's just start walking around. I don't think that smell can be too far away," Gideon said.

Finnie headed off to the left of the cave and Gideon to the right. The bluff curved backwards and Gideon followed along its base. The odor grew stronger with each step until it seemed as if he could taste the stench and he knew that he would be the one that found the source of the smell. The landscape turned rocky, and down in a crevice, Gideon spotted the body of Colin Young. Colin's herding dog lay dead beside the sheepherder. Flies blanketed the remains and an arm looked gnawed on. Gideon spun around and headed to find Finnie.

Finnie had walked back to the horses after realizing that the odor grew fainter in the direction that he had walked.

"I found him. It's not a pretty sight," Gideon said.

"Was he murdered?" Finnie asked.

"I'd say so. His dog is dead too. We'll have to pull him out of a crevice and look at the body," Gideon answered as they mounted their horses.

Gideon would have loved to order Finnie down into the hole to tie a rope around the body, but he couldn't bring himself to do it to his friend. He grabbed his lariat and gloves before maneuvering into the crevice. The air felt stagnant in the hole and the smell nearly intolerable. Slipping a noose around Colin's boots, Gideon tossed the rope up to Finnie.

"Tie the rope onto my saddle horn. Buck's good at pulling," Gideon called out.

The horse pulled the rope, making a grotesque scene as the body slid against the rocks and out of the hole. Gideon dragged the dog out and joined Finnie. The Irishman looked as green as Ireland. He spun around and dropped to his knees before puking. Seeing the vomit proved the final straw for Gideon and he began retching. Neither man stopped until he had lost his lunch.

"We're never going to tell a soul about this," Gideon said after gaining some semblance of composure.

"Don't worry about me. Mary and Abby would never let us live this down. We'd probably have to leave town and start over," Finnie said as he rolled onto his butt and sat upright.

"Let's look him over and get this put to bed," Gideon said as he arose to his feet.

Even with the decomposition of the body, Gideon could see bruising and cuts on Colin's face. Both eyes were blackened and the nose bent at an unnatural angle. Somebody had worked the sheepherder over pretty good before he died. Rolling over the body, they found a bullet hole in the back of the head.

"Somebody beat him until he gave them his money or they decided that there really wasn't any and then they walked him out here and shot him. I think there were at least two of them, maybe three. Colin always wore a gold rope ring. I always noticed it because it seemed such an odd thing on somebody that lived so frugally. They stole it," Gideon said.

"I'd say that's about the size of it. Whoever did this was pretty damn ruthless. That sheepherder suffered before they put him out of his misery," Finnie said.

"That's what I was thinking and makes me worry about what is yet to come," Gideon said.

"What do we do now?" Finnie asked.

"We'll go back to town and get a couple of shovels. We might as well bury Colin here with his dog. I think that's what he'd want. Tomorrow, we'll try to find out who did this," Gideon said.

"I guess I'll be able to add gravedigger to my long list of talents," Finnie remarked.

Telling Mayor Hiram Howard the reason that they needed to borrow a couple of shovels from his store was all that it took for the news of the murder of Colin Young to spread until the whole town was abuzz by the time that Gideon and Finnie returned from burying the sheepherder. Though most of the townsfolk barely knew the man, a begrudging admiration had developed over the years for the hermit and his lifestyle. Last Stand considered Colin as one of their own and therefore the death felt personal. Every conversation in the shops seemed to concern trying to figure out Colin's killer.

Two cowboys sat waiting in the jail when Gideon and Finnie walked into the office. Gideon didn't recognize either man.

"May I help you?" Gideon asked.

"Sheriff, we just returned from driving some cattle to Pagosa Springs and had to stop at the bank to deposit the money for Mr. Dirks. We heard about that sheepherder that got murdered. Last night we stopped at that trading post between here and Pagosa. A couple of rough looking men were in there drinking and they were carrying on about some old hermit sheepherder that wasn't worth their troubles. They never said anything about killing him, but I thought that you should know. They tried to give us some trouble and we wouldn't have it," the taller cowboy said.

"So you two are ranch hands for Kendal Dirks?" Gideon asked.

"Yes, sir," the cowboy answered.

"What did these men look like?" Gideon queried.

"One of them stood about your height and had a walleye. The other one looked tall and skinny and had a front tooth missing. There was a black and a sorrel tied out front. I guess they were theirs. We didn't stay too long," the cowboy answered.

"I appreciate you stopping in. Not everybody would have gone to the trouble. Tell Kendal that I said hi," Gideon said.

After the cowboys took their leave, Finnie said, "What's our plan?"

"There's no point in heading out tonight. We'll leave in the morning. That's too much of a coincidence for them not to be our men. You better sweet talk Mary. We may have to be gone a couple of days. See if she remembers the men that those cowboys described. She wouldn't forget a man with a walleye and another with a front tooth missing," Gideon said.

"She'll get that break from me that she so wanted," Finnie said dejectedly as he plopped down in a chair.

"Quit being such a baby. You know that she was just having some fun with you," Gideon chided.

"I suppose. It'd be nice if she acted as if she appreciated me once in a while when I'm in front of my friends," Finnie said.

"Nothing is more pathetic than an overly sensitive Irishman," Gideon said.

Grinning, Finnie said, "Spoken like a true heartless German. What are we going to do about the sheep?"

"The only other sheepherder that I know of is on the way to Pagosa Springs. We'll see if he'll take them. It's not like there's any kin to inherit the estate anyway," Gideon said.

"Just as long as I don't have to herd them," Finnie said.

"I'm going home. See you in the morning," Gideon said.

Chapter 2

The morning after finding Colin Young's body, Gideon and Finnie met at the jail. They crammed enough hardtack and jerky into their saddlebags for three days as well as plenty of cartridges before heading west on the road to Pagosa Springs.

They weren't a mile out of town before Finnie said, "I know Mary is a lot farther along than last time, but I still worry to death about her. I'd never forgive myself if I was gone and something happened."

"I know you do and I worry about her too, but I wouldn't have asked you to come along if I thought there was a chance that she needed you. She seems to be doing fine this time," Gideon said.

"Doc stopped in the saloon last night and I asked him what he thought. He told me that he felt certain that she was past the danger point," Finnie said.

"Well, you know that old goat wouldn't say that unless he meant it. He thinks a whole lot more of Mary than he does of me or you," Gideon said and grinned.

"When I came to town, Doc was about the last person in the world that I thought I'd become friends with. He's kind of like a boil. He grows on you. I hope age doesn't catch up with him any time soon. The town wouldn't be the same without him," Finnie said.

"He'll probably outlive me and you," Gideon joked.

"Especially considering our line of work. Oh, by the way, Mary didn't recall ever seeing the two men we're looking to find," Finnie said.

"Interesting," Gideon replied.

The trading post sat about sixteen miles from Last Stand at the point where the road turned south at the confluence of the South Fork and Rio Grande rivers. They made good time as they traveled. The road was packed and smooth and only the considerable hills slowed their speed. They reached the post before noon.

South Fork Trading Post had a reputation for dealing with the underbelly of Colorado. Rumors that highwaymen traded their loot there for money persisted. Since becoming sheriff, Gideon had no cause to investigate the post and had never set foot in the establishment.

"Put your badge in your pocket. Maybe they won't know us," Gideon said as they rode up to the post.

The place was empty of people except for a man behind the counter. Gideon and Finnie waited at the door as their eyes adjusted to darkness of the room. The two windows were covered with what passed for curtains and an oil lamp burned low. A path led directly to the counter with little room to roam elsewhere for all the goods stuffed inside the store. The air reeked with staleness from the burning oil and tobacco smoke hovering at the ceiling.

"Can I help you?" the man asked.

The man behind the counter stood a good six feet three inches with a protruding girth. His palms rested on the counter and his arms looked as big as Gideon's thighs. He smelled and looked to have gone a good while without a bath. His dirty, uncombed hair reached his shoulders and fell across his eyes.

"I'm looking for a gold ring," Gideon said.

"Aren't you the sheriff?" the man asked.

"I am," Gideon answered. "I'm looking for a man's gold ring."

"I got a couple for ladies, but that's it. I don't get much jewelry for men," the man said.

"There were two men in here last night. One had a tooth missing and the other had a walleye. What can you tell me about them?" Gideon asked.

The man stood up straight and folded his arms. "You were just trying to see if I had a stolen ring. I don't know nothing about those two fellows you described," he said.

Gideon rubbed the scar on his cheek left from the war and forced a smile. "That's true. I'm just trying to find some men that killed a sheepherder and I think that they were in here last night. I need your help in finding them," he said.

The man's jaw set. He leaned over and pecked Gideon's chest. "I told you that I don't know anything. Now get out of my place," he growled.

With Finnie's fighting ability, he had always been protective of his friends. Pecking Gideon's chest did not sit well with him. Though short in stature, Finnie had shoulders like an ox and he let fly with one of his haymaker right hooks. "Don't touch him," he yelled as his fist connected with the man's jaw.

The man's knees buckled and he grabbed at the counter to keep from going down to the floor. He sucked in a big breath and lunged at Finnie. Finnie grabbed the man by the shirt and yanked the behemoth over the counter as if lifting a feed sack. Gideon jumped back out of the way as Finnie plopped down on the man's chest and started waylaying him.

After a few punches, Gideon said, "That's enough, Finnie. We need him to be able to talk."

"You better tell the sheriff what he wants to know or I'll make you look so bad that your momma won't even love you," Finnie hollered.

Gideon had to cover his mouth to keep from laughing. Finnie had a way with the English language like nobody else he had ever known.

"Okay, I don't know them. They've only been in here a couple of times. I heard them mention having a camp south of here along the river. That's all I know," the man said.

"Now wouldn't talking in the first place have been a lot easier than getting whipped by a little sawed-off shit like me," Finnie said as he climbed off the man's chest.

The man labored to his feet, pinching his nose shut to stop the stream of blood. He didn't say anything else and hurried back behind the counter.

Gideon and Finnie walked outside and mounted their horses. They pinned their badges back on and headed south.

"I appreciate you defending me, but you were a bit impatient about the whole thing. I planned to give him one more chance to back down. If he touched me again, I was going to show him how fast I can draw my Colt and lay it upside his head. I did that to Hank Sligo and he was every bit as big as that guy. Hank wasn't the same for days," Gideon said.

"I have no mercy for bullies. They rile me up but good. I needed the practice anyway," Finnie said, holding up his fist and smiling.

They continued on the trail southwest along the Rio Grande River. After riding about a mile, they topped a ridge and could see a camp in the bend of the river a couple hundred yards away. The two men at the campsite also saw Gideon and Finnie. They mounted their horses and began riding in their direction.

"Do you think they're coming to surrender?" Finnie said in jest.

"I think they are coming to see if we look easy to rob," Gideon said.

"You think?" Finnie said.

"I think," Gideon answered and worked his revolver up and down in its holster until satisfied that it moved smoothly.

The two men rode slow and leisurely towards the lawmen until the two parties had closed to within fifty yards of each other. Gideon and Finnie had the sun to their faces and the other two men apparently saw the light reflecting off their badges. Suddenly, the two men spun their horses around and took off in a gallop.

"Damn it," Finnie yelled as they kicked their horses into a fast lope to pursue the men.

For the first mile, Gideon and Finnie lost ground as the other two men rode in a gallop on the mountain road. Gideon remained confident that it was only a matter of time before the outlaws ran their horses into the ground and then they would catch them. A part of Gideon loved the chase. He locked into the rhythm of his horse and focused on keeping an eye on his quarry. His senses felt hyperactive. The horse sweat smelled pungent and the hoof beats seemed like drums next to his ears. His eyes could see the minutest detail as his mind processed the dangers. The horses of the outlaws began to wear out and slowed dramatically. As Gideon and Finnie rapidly advanced on them, the criminals pulled their revolvers and started firing. The lawmen lowered their heads, but the outlaws were so intent on escaping that they failed to level their guns. Trees were in more danger of taking a bullet than Gideon or Finnie. Closing in on the outlaws, the sheriff and deputy drew their Colts and returned fire. The outlaws made for easy targets at such a close distance and were hit on the first volley. Both men slumped in their saddles. As their weary horses came to a stop, one man slid from the saddle to the ground while the other dropped his gun and grasped the saddle horn.

Gideon and Finnie pulled their horses to a stop and ran towards the men. Finnie yanked the man from the saddle and dragged him to the ground while Gideon checked on the other man.

"This one's dead," Gideon called out.

"This one's alive. He's got one eye looking at me and the other one is checking out the sky," Finnie announced.

The outlaw that remained alive had a hole through the right side of his back and labored to breathe. "I need a doctor," he said.

Gideon paused a moment to gather himself. His mind felt as if a million thoughts were happening all at once. He took a breath and willed calmness. "Yes, you do, and we're a long ways from one. So the sooner you answer my questions, the sooner we leave," he said as he walked over to the outlaw. "Did you two kill Colin Young?"

"Go to hell," the man said.

"I may, but you're going first if you don't get to a doctor and we aren't leaving until you answer my questions," Gideon said.

"Yeah, we killed him. That old hermit didn't have nothing," the man said while gasping for breath.

"What's your name?" Gideon inquired.

"Pete Decker," the man answered.

"Was there anybody else in on it besides you two?" Gideon asked.

The man hesitated before answering. "No, just me and Colby," Pete said.

"Where's the ring?" Finnie asked.

"I don't know nothing about a ring," the outlaw answered.

In a threatening tone, Gideon said, "Where's the ring?"

"I don't know about a ring. Please get me to a doctor," Pete pleaded.

Gideon didn't say anything more, but walked to his horse and retrieved some bandages from his saddlebag. The gunshot had not exited the man's body and Gideon helped Pete roll onto his stomach. He then ripped the shirt and used his finger to shove the dressing up into the wound. Pete screamed as he worked.

"That's about all I can do for you. It should slow the bleeding until Doc has a chance to fix you," Gideon said.

Finnie grabbed an arm and Gideon the other as they pulled Pete to his feet and helped him onto his horse. The Irishman retrieved some leather strips from his saddlebag and tied Pete's hands to the saddle horn and his feet to the stirrups in case the outlaw lost consciousness while riding.

The lawmen tied the other man's body across his saddle and headed for home. They were forced to travel slowly as the jarring caused Pete to groan in pain as he struggled for breath. By the time that they reached the trading post, the outlaw gasped for air and made a gurgling sound with each breath.

"I can't breathe. I can't breathe," Pete yelled. His face revealed sheer terror and a lack of color. He desperately fought the bindings holding him in the saddle as he panicked.

"He's drowning in his own blood," Finnie said.

"And there's not a damn thing that we can do about it. We've seen this before in the war," Gideon remarked.

Pete gave one final effort to break free from his bindings before slumping over the horse's neck. Gideon turned his horse and moved beside Pete's mount. He checked the outlaw's pulse.

"He's gone," Gideon said.

Solemnly, they rearranged the body across the saddle and resumed their journey.

"Are we still going to stop and see that sheepherder about Colin's sheep?" Finnie asked.

"I guess we better. I wish we would've done that on the way down here, but I didn't want to waste time," Gideon said.

"Nothing like dropping in on someone with a couple of bodies in tow," Finnie said.

"Do you ever think that maybe we used our guns too soon instead of trying to take them alive?" Gideon asked.

"Gideon, they were shooting at us. We can't say please stop shooting so that we can arrest you and hang you later. I don't see where we had much of a choice," Finnie said.

"I know, but sometimes I wonder if Saint Peter will pull out this scroll of all the people I've killed and say that I apparently didn't understand the sixth commandment very well and I'm not allowed through the gates. The older I get, the more taking a life bothers me. Life is precious and there was a time when I didn't have much regard for it," Gideon said as he rubbed his scar.

"Neither one of us has taken a life just for the sake of killing someone. There may have been times where you could have used more discretion, but never a time where you were not on the side of right. Somebody has to preserve law and order and I have to believe that's what counts," Finnie said.

Gideon grinned. "My little philosophical Irishman. I suppose you're right," he said.

"I guess this is the end of solving Colin's murder," Finnie said.

"I suppose so, but I don't think that we got to the bottom of things," Gideon said.

"What do you mean?" Finnie asked.

"I think he lied when he said that there were only two of them. Somebody else was in on the killing and that one got the ring, but we don't have anything else to go on. Unless the ring shows up, we're done," Gideon said.

"Any ideas?" Finnie questioned

"No, but I wonder how they found out about Colin Young. They were either in Last Stand and heard someone talking about Colin's money and we didn't know about it or somebody else in town is the ears of the outfit," Gideon said.

"For now, I'd like to assume that this is all over with," Finnie muttered.

Chapter 3

Joann waddled to her new stove. Seven and a half months pregnant with her first child, she began cracking eggs against the skillet. She and her husband Zack had moved into their new cabin a little over a month ago. They had been granted their homestead the previous fall and with the help of Gideon, Ethan Oakes, and others, they had built the cabin after the frost left the ground that spring. The couple had used reward money that Zack had received for his part in capturing the Cooper Gang to furnish their new home and to buy a mule, plow, buckboard, and other things necessary for their homestead.

Joann had been born out of wedlock to Abigail Schone and Gideon, and raised by Abby's aunt and uncle in Wyoming. After Gideon's return to Last Stand, she had finally met her real father and the two had developed a father-daughter bond over time. She had met Zack on her trips to Colorado and the two had married.

"If that ass is ever scrawny again, I'll never complain about it once," Zack teased.

"You're the one that made me this way," Joann shot back.

"I'm responsible for the bump in the front, not the one in the back," he said with a grin.

"Zack Barlow, you could hurt my feelings talking like that. You have no idea how hungry a baby makes me. Abs had three babies and she looks as good as she ever did and I expect I'll be the same, but if you keep running that mouth, you may never get the chance to make me look like this again," she said.

"I don't recall ever having to twist your arm," Zack said.

"Oh, shut up. My daddy found you out in the sticks and he can make you disappear just as easily," Joann warned.

"Gideon loves me more than he does you," he said.

"You're awfully full of yourself today. He does take your side more than I think necessary. I'll give you that," she said begrudgingly.

She finished cooking their breakfast and Zack helped her bring the food to the table. He gave her a kiss as he pulled her chair out for her.

"I do love you," he said.

"I was beginning to wonder with the way that you were talking. What are you going to do today?" Joann asked.

"I'm going to check on the alfalfa and the herd before I cut some trees for the barn. I'd like to have it built by fall. What about you?" Zack said before taking a bite of egg.

Zack had plowed under twenty acres that spring and sown the land in alfalfa to sell hay to the other ranchers. He had worked full-time for Ethan and Sarah Oakes on their ranch until March and now worked for them part-time. Ethan had also sold him fifty heifers and allowed him the use of his bulls to breed his new herd.

"Today is Wednesday. I'm going to go watch Chance so Abs can have her time to be with Sarah and Mary," Joann answered.

Chance was Joann's twenty-month-old baby brother, eighteen years her junior.

"Are you sure you should be riding over there? You're getting awfully far along to get jostled about," he said.

"I'll be fine. Just hitch the horse to the buckboard for me. That big ass you were complaining about gives me plenty of cushion," she said, taking a sip of coffee and grinning mischievously over it.

Zack smiled. "When we were courting and you gave me fits, I should've known I'd never get the last word in," he said.

"True," Joann replied and winked at her husband.

Zack set his fork down on the plate. "What are we going to do if we don't have a clue on how to raise a baby? Neither one of us has any experience except for being around Chance. We don't know what we're doing," he said.

Joann reached across the table and patted her husband's hand. "We'll figure it out. People have been having their first child since the beginning of time and it will all work out. And besides, we have Abs and Sarah to help us. If I had to bet, I'd say we'll be ready to throw them out of here with all the help they'll be offering," she said and smiled.

"I know you're right, but having a baby seems so scary. I've never had to take care of someone else before," Zack said.

"You take plenty good care of me," Joann said, making Zack smile.

After they finished their breakfast, Zack hitched the buckboard and saddled his horse. He walked with Joann to the wagon and helped her climb up to the seat.

"You be careful. I love you," he said.

"Love you too. See you later," she said before coaxing the horse to move.

To lessen the jarring, Joann drove the wagon slowly to the Johann cabin. Abby sat with her daughter, Winnie, swinging on the porch and watching Chance play with their dog as Joann pulled into the yard on the buckboard. Abby walked over and helped her daughter down from the wagon.

"Joann, I must say that being pregnant agrees with you. You look lovely," Abby said.

"Well, Zack told me this morning how big my butt was getting," Joann said.

"He did what?" Abby said.

"Abs, he was only kidding and as much grief as I give that man, I have it coming," Joann said.

"I guess, but that sounds a little rough to me," Abby said.

"Trust me, it was all in fun. You know Zack doesn't have a mean bone in his body," Joann reminded her mother.

Chance toddled over to his sister and she picked him up. Winnie made sure to nestle up against her big sister at seeing her little brother getting some attention.

"Joann," Chance said.

"We're going to have fun while Mommy is gone, aren't we?" Joann said to her brother as she draped an arm around her sister.

"I'm going to go saddle Snuggles and get to town," Abby said and kissed each of her children.

Abby prided herself on her horsemanship and she put Snuggles into a lope after the animal's muscles were warmed. She loved the feel of the wind blowing her hair back and the freedom from motherhood for a few hours. Locking into the rhythm of the horse, she lost herself in daydreams.

The group of women had originally met at Sarah's cabin, but after Doc had refused to allow Mary to travel while pregnant, they had moved to the back room of the saloon. Ethan preached on Sundays and the news that Sarah could be seen going into the saloon on a weekly basis had all the old ladies in Last Stand wearing themselves out with gossip. Sarah had never been one to care what anyone thought about her and made jokes about her notoriety.

Mary and Sarah were already sitting at the table sipping coffee as Abby slipped down the alley and into the saloon from the back door.

"It's about time that you got here," Sarah said. "We were about to attack the cookies without you."

"My babysitter is moving a little slower these days," Abby said.

"Oh, yes, how is Grandma Johann going to keep our get-togethers going after the new arrival?" Sarah asked.

"Sarah Oakes, don't you dare call me that. I'm too young to be a grandma. That baby is going to call me Mimi. I know that I'll love it like all get out, but it could have waited a few more years to make its appearance and I would have loved it just as much," Abby said as Mary and Sarah laughed at her.

"That's what happens when you have a baby so young. They grow up and have babies too," Sarah said.

"I had enough lectures from my parents on that to last a lifetime. Gideon wooed me and I didn't know any better," Abby said with a laugh.

"How is Joann feeling?" Mary asked before biting into a cookie.

"Good. You and her both look so cute pregnant. I wish I were having a baby. Joann, Winnie, and Chance are all so far apart in age that they never got to have a true playmate," Abby said and poured herself a cup of coffee.

"I don't want to hear it. At least you got to have three. I surely would have liked to have had more than Benjamin, though I consider him a miracle. Now that he's older, he doesn't need me like he used to when he was younger. You still have a little one to hold," Sarah said.

"I know, but I feel old knowing that those days of having babies are probably gone for good and a new chapter is starting. And you can come get Chance any time that you want. He about wears me out," Abby said.

"Enough about us. How are you feeling, Mary?" Sarah asked.

"I feel good. The baby kicks me all the time and Finnie about wears me out worrying, but compared to losing one, this is easy," Mary said.

"How is the restaurant doing?" Abby asked.

Finnie and Mary had bought the shutdown Lucky Horse Saloon the previous fall and converted it into a restaurant with elbow grease and more expense than they had ever intended.

"Business is getting better all the time. Especially after we figured out that Delta couldn't work there. Ladies don't like retired whores serving their husbands their meal. They seem to have forgotten or gotten over the fact that I was one. Delta's past is still a little too fresh, I guess. We keep Delta here behind the bar and let Charlotte work the restaurant. If I had known that

I'd get pregnant again this quickly, I would have waited, but we can't change that now," Mary said.

"Now that we have all that out of the way, it's time to start complaining about our husbands," Abby said before grabbing a cookie from the tray and taking a bite.

"It won't be long before Abby can tell us what it's like to sleep with a grandfather," Sarah said, making Mary snort with laughter and Abby to spit cookie.

Chapter 4

As Kurt Tanner cut a calf from the herd, Ethan sat back on his mount and watched with admiration as the rider and horse worked together flawlessly. Kurt had arrived in Last Stand during the winter needing a job. The feed store had hired him and he soon earned the reputation of a hard worker. After Zack decided that he could only work part-time for Ethan, the rancher had hired Kurt to replace him. The arrangement had worked out well. Two men could not keep up with all that needed tending to on the ranch, but with Ethan and Kurt working full-time, and Zack part-time, the ranch ran like a clock.

Kurt sent his rope sailing over the calf's neck and Ethan lassoed the rear legs. As the ranch hand threw the animal to the ground, Ethan placed the brand against the hide. The pungent smell of burning hair and hide wafted through the air. Ethan never got used to the smell. On some days, it nearly gagged him and he gladly tossed the brand to the ground, happy that they were finished for the day.

"Let's call it a day. Sarah said that she planned on making dumplings. Why don't you have supper with us tonight?" Ethan said.

"Thank you, Mr. Oakes. I'm much obliged. That sure sounds good and my belly is telling me that it's ready for some food," Kurt said.

The two men rode back to Ethan's cabin where they found Sarah standing at the stove cooking and Benjamin reading a book at the table. After Gideon and Zack had arrived in Last Stand, Benjamin had idolized the two men and they adored him. The same could not be said for his relationship with Kurt. The young man's attempts to bond with the boy proved so awkward as to be painful to watch. Sarah, on the other hand, had been smitten by Kurt. The twenty-one-year-old man had obviously not had much of an upbringing and Sarah felt determined to help him smooth out his rough edges.

"You two look good and hungry. Supper will be ready by the time that you wash up," Sarah said.

Ethan and Kurt scrubbed their hands and returned to the table.

"What are you reading?" Kurt asked Benjamin.

"The Adventures of Tom Sawyer," Benjamin answered.

"Oh," Kurt said. He could barely read and had never heard of the book. His mind went blank on what else to say.

Sarah ordered Benjamin to set the table and when the boy finished, she brought the steaming dumplings to the table and dished a helping into each of the plates. Ethan gave the blessing and they all began eating.

"So how do you like Last Stand?" Sarah asked Kurt.

"I like it pretty good and the people are nice. Everybody seems to have accepted me," Kurt said.

"That's good to hear. Maybe you'll find you a girl and settle down in Last Stand one of these days," Sarah said.

"I don't know, ma'am. I don't cross paths with too many girls," Kurt said.

"You need to come to church with us on Sunday. There's some fine young ladies that come to hear Ethan preach," Sarah said.

"I'll have to think about that, ma'am. I've never been much for church and such," Kurt said.

Ethan looked at Kurt. "Don't let Sarah talk you into something that you're not ready to try. You'll know when you are ready. Sarah is always trying to marry off every bachelor in the county and she tries to grow the church with the results," he said.

"Ethan Oakes, I was just trying to tell Kurt where he could find some girls of high moral character," Sarah said.

"You just want everybody in the chains of marriage," Ethan said and grinned at his wife.

"I'll make you think chains of marriage when I chain you to a raft and send you down river. The ocean probably wouldn't take you," Sarah said.

"She likes to show off," Ethan said.

"I appreciate Miss Sarah looking out for me. I really do," Kurt said before concentrating on eating his food and trying to stay out of the conversation.

Benjamin began entertaining with the tales of Tom Sawyer. He had everybody laughing and envisioned himself an adult with his newfound command of the dinner table. He watched his ma and pa as they listened to the stories and felt like their equal.

Sarah covertly watched Kurt eat. He held his eating utensils like shovels and attacked his plate as if he were digging for gold. She really liked the young man and hoped that she would have the opportunity to refine his manners. In her mind, all Kurt needed was a little guidance to become a respectable part of the community.

After the meal, Kurt quickly excused himself and rode to the cabin that Ethan provided for him. He had moved there after Zack and Joann had left the place to live in their new cabin. Retrieving a bucket of water from the well, he went inside and washed himself before putting on clean clothes. Plopping down onto his bed, he drifted off to sleep for an hour and then rode to town. Most nights he frequented the Last Stand Last Chance Saloon.

Kurt walked into the saloon and Mary smiled from behind the bar when she caught sight of him. She liked the cowboy and his harmless flirting with her. He seemed like a nice young man that had managed to raise himself above a difficult start to life. Nobody in Last Stand could relate to humble beginnings more than she could with her childhood spent in an orphanage.

"You get prettier every time I come in here," Kurt said. "I'll have a beer if you please."

"You must like the looks of a woman with child then," Mary said as she retrieved a mug.

"You look happy. That's what matters," he said.

"Yes, you are right about that. I am happy. How's working for Ethan going?" she asked.

"Good. That's a fine family and Ethan is easy to work with. I'm terrible with kids though and I haven't exactly won over Benjamin," Kurt said.

You're probably trying too hard. Just be yourself and don't treat him like a little boy. Benjamin is mature beyond a normal eleven-year-old," Mary said.

"I'll remember that. I do like him," Kurt said.

"We all think he's pretty special," she said.

"I heard that your husband and the sheriff killed the men that murdered that sheepherder," he said.

"Yes, unfortunately they had no choice. Three people are dead and nobody has anything to show for it," Mary said.

"That is a shame. At least they solved the murder and made things safer around here," Kurt said and took a sip of beer.

"That they did. It just doesn't do poor old Colin Young any good," she said.

"No, it doesn't. It's always nice talking to you, Mary. I think I'll go see if I can rustle me up a card game," he said before walking over to a table where a couple of other ranch hands sat and pulled up a seat with them.

Mary had noticed that Kurt always avoided the high stakes games with seasoned players. He instead chose to play against ranch hands for little pots that he nearly always won before the night was finished. Kurt certainly didn't get rich off his winnings, but he made enough to pay for his evening and he was smart enough to buy the players a drink when the game finished.

Gideon walked into the saloon. He had ridden to town in the afternoon after spending the morning tending to his herd. On days that he came in late, he liked to stay in Last Stand into the evening so that the town knew that he occasionally worked nights.

"I figured I'd see you in here," Mary said and poured Gideon a beer without him asking.

"I figured if I didn't work tonight, I'd have to listen to your husband complaining in the morning about how he has to carry me," Gideon said.

"That sounds about right," she said.

"Where is Finnie?" Gideon asked.

"He's upstairs. I have no idea what he's doing," Mary said.

"I guess I should be happy and let my ears rest," he said.

"Be nice. You'd be lost without him," she said.

Gideon grinned. "Like you don't pick on him too and you're married to that gabby little man," he said. "What do you think of Kurt?"

"I like him. He kind of reminds me of myself. I can tell that he's had a rough childhood and he's trying to make something of himself. I think he's a good one," Mary said.

"I don't know. There's something about him that doesn't strike me right – as if he's hiding a secret. Just a feeling I get," Gideon said.

"What's the matter? Are you afraid that Ethan is going to get a new best friend and replace you?" she teased.

Giving Mary a condescending look, he said, "No, just an intuition I have about Kurt."

"Gideon, I'm the one with intuition about people and I'm always right. You, not so much," Mary said.

"Yes, Mary, we all know how you can size up the good or evil in men with a single glance. You remind us enough," Gideon said.

"You are never going to get over the fact that I can always tell what you're thinking or know when something is troubling you, are you?" she asked.

"Probably not. It's annoying. You're annoying," Gideon said and grinned.

"But you love me anyway," Mary said.

"I have to. You did save my life," he said.

Finnie walked down the stairs and Mary spotted him.

"Hey Finnie, Gideon wants to hear all about our plans for the baby. I need to sit down and rest. Delta can bartend," Mary said and gave Gideon a devilish grin before retreating to the back room.

Chapter 5

Having made a morning walk of the town, Gideon headed back towards the jail. As he neared his office, he saw the rancher, Carter Mason, enter the building. Gideon quickened his pace and found Carter sitting in a chair and Finnie talking with him.

"Hello, Carter. Is Colin's flock on you again? I asked Leo Stewart to take them," Gideon said.

Carter looked agitated and started twisting the end of his mustache. "No, Sheriff, something worse. I have a herd missing. They were grazing on the east side of the ranch and we hadn't checked on them for a few days. I'm no tracker, but the boys and I think there were three sets of horse tracks," he said.

"I'm sorry to hear that. You've had a run of bad luck lately," Gideon said.

"Not as bad as Colin did, but bad enough. Nothing riles me up like rustlers. I'd hang them on the spot if I caught them," Carter said.

"So you don't really know what day they went missing?" Gideon asked.

"Not really. We don't check each herd every day," Carter said.

"Finnie and I will ride out there with you and you can show us where the herd was," Gideon said.

"Much obliged, Sheriff. I hate being such a burden, but I didn't see much choice in the matter," Carter said.

"That's why they pay us. Keeps me in a job," Gideon said.

Carter led them to the corner of his property where the herd had last been grazing. After following the tracks far enough to get away from the marks of Carter's crew, Gideon concluded that Carter had been right in his count of three rustlers. The rancher headed back to his home after having to be convinced that he no longer was needed.

"We're going to spend all day riding and end up at the railyard in Alamosa. I'd bet on it," Gideon said.

"I thought that too. We've seen it before," Finnie said.

"I thought our rustlers had moved on or Colin's killers might have been them, but this looks like the same thing we saw this spring. And I still think that the livestock clerk that works for the Denver and Rio Grande Railroad is a crook. He's either part of some rustling syndicate or he takes bribes to look the other way. Same for that railroad detective they've got running around there. He's as useless as tits on a boar hog," Gideon said and spit on the ground.

"I think that detective just don't like us because he fought for the Confederacy and we fought for the Union. He'll never quit fighting that war," Finnie said.

"Either way, we're not going to get any cooperation when we get there and there's never enough evidence to get a warrant. And the two times that I wired the Denver sheriff to check the railyards there for the brands of stolen cattle, he came up empty. I just don't know," Gideon said.

The Denver and Rio Grande Railroad had reached Alamosa, Colorado in 1878 and had been a boon to everybody in the vicinity. Ranchers could now ship their cattle to market if they so desired instead of making cattle drives, and storeowners had a much easier time getting goods from Denver. Unfortunately, riffraff, gamblers, rustlers, and other undesirables always followed the railroad tracks.

"Do you think we're in for a run of trouble?" Finnie asked.

"I wouldn't doubt it. I've seen this happen before. The railroad comes to town and so do the thieves and such. After a while, either the town gets fed up with the crime and the sheriff straightens things up or a group of vigilantes will hang a few of the worst ones. Some of Alamosa's finest hooded citizens just hanged a couple of men that killed a blacksmith. They decided not to wait for a trial. Every town needs a good smithy and they apparently got riled up when they lost theirs. The next thing you know, some of the riffraff will hop the train for greener pastures and some will wander out to a nearby town. That town could be Last Stand," Gideon said.

The trail the herd had been driven down ran parallel to the road between the towns, but always stayed out of sight of the thoroughfare. Most of the land was open range pasture with some ridges and valleys to navigate. Mountains jutted out to both the north and south.

Gideon noticed that one set of horse tracks veered off back towards the road. He watched for another mile to see if the tracks came back to the heard and could not find any sign of them.

"One of the riders went to the road and either rode back to Last Stand or on to Alamosa," Gideon said.

"What do you think that is about?" Finnie asked.

"I couldn't really say. I'd guess they either went on ahead to make arrangements or they needed to be back in Last Stand," Gideon said.

"This is all a bit queer," Finnie mused.

"Let's push on into Alamosa and to the railyard. That's where these tracks are headed," Gideon said and put Buck into a lope.

They hitched their horses at the railyard and walked into the rail office. Gideon found the same livestock clerk that he had dealt with in the past sitting at his desk. Gideon rubbed his hands together to help suppress the urge to walk up and bounce the railroad employee's nose off the desk until the clerk's condescending attitude had bled away.

"Can I help you?" the clerk asked.

"I'm tracking a herd of cattle that were stolen and brought here. I believe there was about a hundred head brought here in the last three days. Three men were driving them," Gideon said.

"We've had cattle brought in, but that's about as much as I can tell you," the clerk said.

"Can I have the names of men that had cattle shipped?" Gideon asked.

"The Denver and Rio Grande Railroad is not in the habit of sharing business transactions with the law without a warrant. I'm sorry that I cannot help you, but I'm just following company policy," the clerk said.

"You should come visit Last Stand sometime. I'd love to show you around," Gideon said before spinning around and walking out the door.

Gideon and Finnie walked around the railyard until they saw the rail detective limping across the tracks towards them. He was dressed in his ever-present overcoat that he wore no matter the weather and a bowler hat shoved down to his eyebrows.

"I see that the Yankees from Last Stand are snooping around again," the detective said.

"I have a herd of stolen cattle that ended up here. Did you see a herd of about a hundred come in in the last three days?" Gideon asked.

"I see cattle all the time. How am I supposed to tell the stolen ones from the others? If you Union boys can do that, well, then you're smarter than me," the detective said.

"You know that war ended seventeen years ago. Don't you think that it's time to let it go?" Gideon asked.

"Not if you saw what you did to my home and my way of life," the detective answered.

"We were all just following orders. I try not to think about those days. Can you provide me any information?" Gideon said, trying not to antagonize the detective.

"Do you know for a fact that they came here?" the detective asked.

"We tracked them until about a mile from Alamosa and then all the newer cattle tracks wiped them out, but I feel certain they came here," Gideon said.

"That's too bad. I guess no judge will give you a warrant based on what you think happened," the detective said.

Finnie took a step towards the detective. "Why don't you give me your best shot? I'd love to have a go at you," he said.

The detective leaned down into Finnie's face. "You boys need to get out of here. I'm the law here," he said.

"Come on, Finnie. This is useless," Gideon said and tugged on his deputy's arm to get him away.

They rode to the jail and found the sheriff of Alamosa sitting at his desk. The sheriff stood about Gideon's height and his chubbiness gave the impression that he was too soft for the job. Gideon had met Sheriff White twice before and came away with the impression that the lawman was an honest man but somewhat overwhelmed with his job.

"Sheriff Johann, what brings you to town?" Sheriff White asked as a way of a greeting.

"We had a herd rustled back at Last Stand and I'm pretty sure the cattle were driven to the railyard and shipped, but I can't get any cooperation down there. I was hoping that you might have some leads on some rustlers," Gideon said.

"I got rustlers around here, just no leads on them, and that detective down at the railyard needs a club laid upside his head. I'm afraid I'm not much information and I got my hands full around here. Half the town is mad at me that the two killers got lynched and the other half mad that they felt like that they had to take matters into their own hands. I'm getting telegrams from the governor wondering what's going on down here. Sorry that I can't be of more help," the sheriff said.

Gideon felt sorry for the sheriff. The poor guy looked as if he was at his wits' end and Gideon didn't have any advice for him. Some people were cut out to be sheriff and some weren't. "Thank you for your time. I hope things get better for you," he said.

As they walked out of the jail, Finnie grumbled, "I might as well have stayed in bed all day. I would have got just as much done."

"But you would have missed out on the pleasure of my company and a ride out into the country. We've had worse days," Gideon said.

"Aye, that we have," Finnie said.

On the ride home, they stopped at a couple of ranches that sat in view from the road. The ranchers had seen a couple of herds of cattle being driven, but neither could provide any useful information. Gideon and Finnie returned to Last Stand late in the day feeling that the trip had been a waste.

"What do we do now?" Finnie asked.

"Somebody will notice that their herd has been stolen before the rustlers have a chance to get away. It's just a matter of time," Gideon said.

"Hope you're right. I think I should just become a bartender," Finnie said. "It fits my temperament and I wouldn't be traveling all day."

"I'd bet you'd be more likely to get shot by Mary if you were bartending than by outlaws being a deputy," Gideon said.

"I'm too tired to argue with you. My belly is more concerned with getting fed than my mind is with debating you. I'll see you later," Finnie said as he rode on to the livery stable and left Gideon in front of the jail.

Chapter 6

Doc sat in the saloon nursing a second beer after the lunch crowd had thinned out until only two other patrons remained. He needed to get back to the office in case a patient arrived, but he wanted to talk with Mary. She finished helping Delta clear away the food and plates before walking over to the table and sitting down with the doctor.

"What's going on?" Mary asked.

"Mary, you know that John and his family arrive on the stage at three o'clock today and I'm as nervous as a cat in a rocking chair factory," Doc said.

John Hamilton was Doc's son that had been born out of wedlock while the doctor attended medical school in Boston. The family of John's mother had been one of the wealthiest in Boston and had used their resources to prevent Doc from ever seeing his child. Doc had eventually given up on ever meeting his son and moved out west. Last fall, John had arrived in Last Stand unannounced and met his father for the first time. The two men had bonded and now John planned to return with his wife and three children.

"Doc, I've seen you worry yourself to death about a patient, but I've never known you to get riled up about much of anything else," she said.

"This is different. I'll be sixty-nine years old in a couple of months and meeting John last year was the shock of a lifetime, but I never had time to think about it. I've been thinking about this for two months. John understands why I never got to see him. What if Kate and the children don't? They may hate me," he said.

John had kept his identity a secret upon his arrival in Last Stand until he was accidently shot in a barroom fight between two other men. Doc had learned that John was his son as he was about to perform surgery to save his offspring's life.

"From what John said, Kate is a strong-willed woman. I doubt she would make the trip if she felt that way. The children are young enough that they will judge you on who you are and not the past. I think you're getting yourself worked up for nothing," Mary said.

"I guess we're about to find out," he said before taking a swig of beer.

"This whole town loves you. Just be your grouchy old self and I'm sure they'll love you too," she said with a smile and a pat on Doc's hand.

"You know one thing that has always galled me? It's listening to people talk about their grandkids. I always wonder if their life is so pathetic that grandkids are the only reason they have to live. It seems like a sad state of affairs to me. What if I don't even like these kids? They've all had birthdays since John last visited and I sent them money. Nothing like trying to buy some love. Henry is seventeen, Rose is fourteen, and Tad is four. The oldest two will probably be at that age where they don't like anyone," Doc said.

"Doc, I'm about to have my first child so I'm no expert on the subject, but if I were betting, I'd say that's the least of your concerns. I have a feeling that by the time that they leave, you'll have a whole new perspective on the subject," Mary said.

Doc smiled for the first time. "Maybe you're right. Worrying won't change anything anyways. Thank you for our talk. You're pretty handy to have around," he said.

Mary stood and awkwardly bent over using her hands to support her stomach. She kissed the doctor's cheek. "You've been pretty handy to have around a time or two yourself," she said.

Drinking the last of his beer in one gulp, Doc shuffled out of the Last Chance and back to his office. He treated two patients before closing his practice at two-thirty and hanging a sign on his door. Looking at himself in the mirror, he grabbed a comb and ran it through his hair before walking down to where the stage arrived. He sat down on the bench, pulled out his pocket watch to check the time, and waited.

The stage appeared from down the street. Doc could feel his heart thumping in his chest and he felt lightheaded. He couldn't remember the last time that he'd let himself get so worked up and he tried to focus on the conversation that he had with Mary. As the cloud of dust drifted away from the stopped stage, Doc saw John and he assumed Kate smiling at him. Seeing John dressed in the ranch clothes he had purchased in Last Stand on his previous visit made the doctor smile.

John jumped out of the coach and helped Kate and the two youngest children down before the oldest son emerged. Doc stood taking in the features of the fine looking family as they gathered themselves. He ran each child's name through his mind one more time for fear of forgetting it. His son came at him like a bear and embraced him.

"Father, it is so good to see you again. You're looking well," John said before releasing the doctor. "This is Kate, Henry, Rose, and Tad."

Before Doc could speak, Kate rushed over and kissed his cheek.

"I hear that you are not only a fine father, but you come in pretty handy as a doctor as well. I thank you for saving John's life," Kate said.

"I didn't have much choice in the matter if I wanted to hear the whole story about him," Doc said with a smile. "It's good to meet you, Kate."

Sizing up the children, Doc could see that the oldest, Henry, stood back and seemed reserved. The boy already stood taller than his father and resembled his grandfather on the maternal side of the family. He would be the difficult one to win over. The younger two seemed bursting at the seams to meet their grandfather.

"Can we call you Grandpa?" Rose asked. Her excitement caused her to bounce about in front of Doc.

"I hadn't thought about that. You can call me whatever you want. It may take me awhile to realize that you're talking to me. I've been called Doc for so long, I've about forgot my own name," Doc said.

Rose gave Doc a hug around the waist, and Tad, seeing his sister's actions, grabbed the doctor around the leg. Taken aback by the moment, Doc set his jaw to keep from betraying his feelings. The welcoming proved more than he could have hoped for and he felt himself getting misty and growing sentimental over being a grandfather.

Doc held his hand out to Henry and they shook.

"Henry, I'm glad to have the opportunity to meet you. Your father told me a lot about you and I can see now why he is so proud," Doc said.

"Thank you, sir. Nice to meet you too. We have all enjoyed the sights on our travel out here," Henry said a bit stiffly.

"This is God's country. It gets into your blood. Last Stand is nothing like Boston, that's for sure," Doc said.

John and Henry grabbed the large luggage and Doc and Kate retrieved a couple of smaller bags before they walked to the hotel.

After they checked in, Doc said, "So, do you need to rest or would you like to see the town?"

Realizing that her two younger children needed to expend some energy, Kate said, "Show us around the town. I didn't ride that train all this way to sit in a hotel."

"My pleasure," Doc said.

As they walked out of the hotel, Kate hooked her arm into Doc's arm. The family walked down the sidewalk towards the doctor's office.

Kate pointed across the street at the Last Chance. "Is that the saloon where you were shot?' she asked.

John grinned. "It was," he said.

"I see you told her the whole story. If it's any consolation, we haven't had a shooting in there since that night. How is the shoulder feeling?" Doc asked.

"Fine. It hurts just enough now and then to remind me that I got shot and gives me an excuse to tell the story again. If I had a dollar for every time I've told it, I could retire," John said.

"With each telling, his injury gets more direr than the last. I expect him to say he died one of these days," Kate said with a mischievous grin.

Doc smiled at Kate. He was already starting to like her. "Imagine how I felt. I learned he was my son just before I put him under. I was so beside myself that I didn't know if I could retrieve the bullet. Thank goodness Mary was there. Her presence helped," he said.

"How is Mary?" John asked.

"You should see her. She's with child again and she's going to carry this one," Doc said, failing to conceal his fondness for the expectant mother-to-be.

"She must be special. I've heard enough about her and all these other western women to be jealous," Kate said.

"John and I prefer eastern women," Doc said.

Kate laughed. "Good answer. You are charming," she said.

Once at the doctor's office, Doc let the two youngest children listen to their heartbeats with his stethoscope and gave them suckers from his jar. The medical equipment and supplies piqued Henry's curiosity and he roamed around the room looking at them.

"Have you treated many gunshot wounds?" Henry asked, his enthusiasm causing him to lose his formality.

"I've treated my fair share. After the war, Last Stand turned into a rough place until Sheriff Fuller cleaned up the town. And I still have more gunshots than I wish I did. People can be evil," Doc said.

"I'm sure that it must feel very rewarding to save someone's life," Henry said.

"Do you have an interest in medicine?" Doc asked.

Henry grinned at his father. "I think I've been groomed for a life in banking," he said.

"I never said that. I just taught you what I know," John said.

"A lifetime lasts too long to do a job that you don't love," Doc said. "Let's go over to the jail."

Gideon and Finnie were sitting in their chairs carrying on a lively debate on whether Mary would have a boy or a girl when Doc walked in with his family. The sheriff felt sure that the baby would be a girl while Finnie remained convinced that the child would be a boy. Doc made the introductions. John, having already known the two men, eagerly shook their hands and Henry did the same.

Finnie walked over to Kate and Rose and took each of them by the hand. "Well, aren't you two ladies lovely. John always talked about how mean you were, but I can see that you're much too beautiful for it to be so. I believe you must have some Irish in your blood to be so lovely," he said in his thickest Irish accent.

Kate laughed at him. "I've been warned about you, but you're charming nonetheless," she said.

"You need to talk to Mary then. His charm wears off pretty quickly once you get to know him," Gideon deadpanned.

"I'm just a simple Irishman that appreciates the company of the female persuasion," Finnie said to laughter.

Henry stared at Gideon's revolver. "May I see your gun?" he asked.

Gideon glanced over at John and Kate. John nodded his head. Pulling the weapon from its holster, Gideon unloaded the pistol and handed it to Henry.

"It's heavier than I imagined," Henry said as he carefully looked over the gun.

"That there is a Colt Frontier. Best revolver they ever made," Gideon said.

"Have you ever killed anybody with it?" Henry asked.

"Henry," John admonished.

"It's okay," Gideon said before taking a breath and blowing out the air. "I have. It's nothing I take pleasure in doing. Taking a man's life is a terrible thing, but sometimes it comes with the job. I hope at my day of reckoning that the good Lord takes things into consideration."

Handing the gun back to Gideon, Henry asked, "Do you think there is a chance that I can shoot it before we go back east?"

"If your ma and pa don't care, I'm sure we can make that happen," Gideon said.

"I get to go first," John said.

"Great, my son will be dressing like John and all you other cowboys out here in the west by the time we go back home," Kate said and smiled.

"Hey, kids, come back here with me and I'll lock you in the cell that housed James Cooper. Finnie and I captured him. I also locked my daughter in there one time when she misbehaved," Gideon said as he led Rose and Tad to the cell room.

"Did you really lock your daughter in here?" Rose asked as Gideon closed the cell door and locked it.

"I did until she calmed down some," Gideon said.

"We better be good while we are here or Mom will have you locking us up in there. She can get pretty mad sometimes," Rose announced.

"Well, moms have to keep law and order around the house," Gideon said as he let them out.

Kate walked over to her two youngest children and put a hand on each of their shoulders. "Alright, kids, we need to go to the hotel and clean up before dinner. I'm sure Gideon and Finnie have more important things that they need to do other than entertain us," she said.

As they headed out the door, Finnie said, "Now remember, Kate, if you get tired of John, there's always a place for a lovely thing as yourself here in Last Stand."

Shaking her head and grinning, Kate said, "I'm surprised Mary isn't having that baby in a jail cell. I believe I'd have already shot a flirt like you before now if you were my husband." She whisked out the door before Finnie had time to respond.

Chapter 7

Eating breakfast at a leisurely pace for a change, Gideon listened as Winnie rambled on about her plans for the day. His stepdaughter explained in great detail her intentions for rearranging her room. If Winnie ever finished talking, Gideon planned to saddle the horses so that he and Abby could ride to look at their herd before he headed to the jail. Abby finally sent Winnie off to begin working on her project to end the conversation.

After Abby dressed Chance, she carried him outside and handed him up to Gideon sitting in the saddle. He plopped the child between him and the saddle horn. Chance was already an old hand at riding and contentedly looked around at his surroundings. Abby mounted her horse and they rode out.

"We wouldn't have gotten out of the cabin before noon if I hadn't ended the conversation," Abby said after they rode awhile.

"Winnie certainly was excited about her plans," Gideon said.

"Don't you wish we had another one?" Abby said.

"A baby?" Gideon asked.

"Yes, a baby. Chance could have a playmate," she said.

"I don't think about it. If we have one, I'll be fine, and if we don't, I'm grateful for Chance. And besides, Chance will soon have his own nephew or niece to play with. They'll be like siblings," he said.

"I know, but it makes me feel old to know there might not be another one and that we are going to be grandparents. We're too young," Abby said.

"Apparently not," Gideon said and smiled at her.

"Smile like a fool at me, but we're getting old," she said.

Turning serious, Gideon said, "As long as I get old with you, I'll take it."

"Getting all sentimental on me doesn't make me feel any younger, but it sounds sweet. We still might have one yet. I'm not that old," Abby said.

"I promise I'll do my part as often as you want," Gideon said and grinned.

"Of that I can be assured," she said as they reached the herd.

"I don't know why we keep the herd. I don't have the time to take care of them the way I should. If Ethan and Zack didn't come over here and help me, we'd really be in a bind. The hiring of the bottom of the barrel help when we need it doesn't work very well," Gideon mused.

"I love having the herd and riding out here with Chance to check on them. I still think we need a couple hundred more head and then hire a fulltime ranch hand. I could play foreman. Bossing someone around suits my style," Abby said, grinning.

"I won't argue with that last part. Maybe you're right. We wouldn't get rich on it," he said.

"As long as we make a little is all that matters. I know that you're not ready to give up being sheriff yet, but I don't want you doing it when you get older. We could build the herd up for when you're ready to take over things," she said.

"You've got it all figured out, don't you?" Gideon asked.

Abby smiled. "I do. I'm what they call the brains of the operation," she said.

Gideon chuckled. "Alright, I'll keep my ear out for any cattle for sale. We'll probably have to buy heifers in the fall," he said.

"Good. Finding the right ranch hand will probably be harder than finding the cows. The herd does look good. I think this year's calves are the best we've produced," Abby said.

"If you say so. You're the foreman. I need to get to town," Gideon said as he swung his horse around.

"Cows," Chance said as he tried to look back at the herd as they rode away.

After taking time to help Winnie move her bed and dresser, Gideon headed for town. Buck had traveled the road so often that Gideon could have slept in the saddle and still ended up at the jail. Finnie sat in front of the jailhouse whittling on a stick as Gideon rode up.

"Top of the morning to you. At least what's left of it," Finnie said.

"I can see that you're keeping the town well protected in my absence. I guess you could poke somebody's eye out with your stick if trouble arose," Gideon said and nodded at the whittling.

"The legend of Gideon Johann does all the work. I can just sit here and amuse myself," Finnie said.

"Amusing you are," Gideon said as he climbed off the horse and walked into the jail with Finnie following at his heels.

Finnie dropped into a chair. "On a serious note, I have kept a close watch on things and nobody new has showed up in town," he said.

"Good. I don't think we have anything to worry about. Those train robbers could be anywhere, but I doubt they'll be heading into any towns for a while," Gideon said.

Three days prior, Gideon had received a telegram concerning a robbery of a Denver and Rio Grande train at a water stop between Alamosa and Pueblo. A passenger had been murdered and the robbers made off with a large haul of money. The men had worn masks and did not seem to fit the description of any known outlaws. By the time a posse arrived, the trail had gone cold to the point that they could not determine which direction the robbers had headed.

"I'll be glad when Mary has the baby. This waiting is about killing me," Finnie said.

"Do you have names picked out yet?" Gideon asked.

"Depends on when you ask. Mary changes her mind every other day and I don't appear to have much say in the matter," Finnie said and sighed.

Gideon grinned at the Irishman. "That's hard to imagine. Who would have thought back in the days when we were two kids fighting in that godawful war that we'd be sitting here today talking about babies and wives?" he asked.

"I didn't think we'd even be alive, let alone have families," Finnie remarked just before Blackie and Zack burst into the jail.

Surprised and a little alarmed at seeing his son-in-law, Gideon asked, "Zack what are you doing in town?"

"Blackie was shoeing my horse. We just saw five riders come into town. Two went into the bank and the other three are standing around outside of it. They look pretty fidgety," Zack said.

"Oh, hell," Gideon said before taking a big breath and puffing up his cheeks as he exhaled. He rubbed his scar and looked around at the other men. "Can you two help?"

Zack nodded his head.

Blackie said, "You better give me a shotgun. My eyesight ain't what it used to be."

Finnie had already jumped up and started retrieving guns and ammo from the rack. He grabbed a flour sack that they kept around for carrying hardtack and dumped shotgun shells into it before handing it and a shotgun to Blackie. The other three men grabbed a Winchester 73.

The bank set on a corner two blocks down from the jail.

Gideon shoved his hat on and worked his pistol up and down in its holster. "Zack and I will go back a block behind the jail and then walk down the street until we come to the side street the bank sits on. Blackie and Finnie, I want you two to cross the street and head towards the bank. Give us a couple minutes so we converge at the same time. Make sure that you pick a spot where you can take cover," he warned.

Leaving Blackie and Finnie waiting in the office, Gideon and Zack walked to the street behind the jail and then in the direction of the bank until they came to the side street that the building faced. Peeking around the corner, Gideon could see the three men lurking in front of the bank door.

"You stay here and I'm going to cross the street and take cover behind the dry goods store. Be careful. You have a baby on the way and I want it to have a daddy," Gideon instructed.

Putting his badge in his pocket, Gideon carried the Winchester against the length of his leg as he crossed the street as nonchalantly as possible. He could feel the outlaws watching him, but made it to the other side without arousing suspicion.

From behind the corner, Gideon glanced down the street. The outlaws no longer watched in his direction, but instead focused their attention on the main street. They had spotted Finnie and Blackie and raised their guns. Gideon took aim on the nearest outlaw.

"Throw down your guns and surrender. You're surrounded," Gideon yelled.

The three men jerked their heads around in Gideon's direction. One of the outlaws swung his rifle towards the sheriff and as he aimed, Gideon fired. The shot hit the man squarely in the chest and he took two steps backwards before collapsing. Darting around the corner, the other two outlaws disappeared from Gideon and Zack's sight.

With their guns blazing, the outlaws ran towards Finnie and Blackie. Finnie dived behind a water trough, but Blackie stood firm and took aim. The roar of the shotgun reverberated off the buildings as the nearest outlaw flew off his feet like a frog hopping through the air and landed on his back. Blackie spun around from taking a bullet, and losing his balance, he fell to the ground. Seeing the blacksmith lying vulnerable on the ground, Finnie took a breath, drew his Colt, and jumped up firing his gun. He and the outlaw stood no more than twenty-five feet apart shooting at each other. Finnie swore he could feel the heat of the bullets flying by his head and expected to die at any moment. Even as he fired his gun, he thought about Mary and the baby. The outlaw suddenly stopped shooting and dropped his gun. He stared Finnie in the eyes before his knees buckled and he toppled over onto his face.

Finnie looked down at himself expecting to see blood. He found none and ran to Blackie. The blacksmith wobbled to his feet and Finnie tugged him behind the water trough.

"My arm don't work so good," Blackie said.

Untying his bandana, Finnie tied the kerchief around the wound. "Just sit still until this is over with and Doc can fix you up. We still got two more to worry about," he said.

"Do you think I'm going to die, Finnie?" Blackie asked. His words sounded strangely unemotional for such a serious question and he looked up at the sky as if watching ducks migrate.

"No, you'll be fine. I promise. Just stay down," Finnie said. He could see that Blackie's eyes looked glassy and he appeared to be in shock.

The town had grown eerily silent and the streets were so empty of people that it could have passed for a ghost town. Shattering the silence, a single shot sounded from inside the bank. The door to the bank flung open and a young woman was forced into the entrance with a man's arm wrapped around her throat.

"Sheriff, I just killed your banker so that you know that I'm serious. If you want this pretty little thing to live to see another day, you and your men are going to throw down your guns and let us ride away," the outlaw yelled.

The news of Mr. Fredrick's death hit Gideon like a punch in the gut. The banker was a well-liked pillar of the community. He had become bank president after a scandal and had turned the bank into a much friendlier place to do business than his predecessor had been willing to do.

Trying to identify the girl proved difficult from the distance of a city block with the additional hindrance of the outlaw's arm partially obscuring the girl's face, but Gideon thought that she was Betsy Gray. The girl was the same age as Joann and the two women were friendly through attending Ethan's church.

"If you kill her, you'll be a dead man for sure," Gideon yelled back.

"I'll be a dead man for sure if I try to ride out of here without her. I'm dead either way unless you throw down your guns and let us leave. I've got nothing to lose," the outlaw hollered.

"I'll walk to you and you can take me instead of the girl," Gideon called out.

"No, sir. I've heard about you. I already made a mistake in robbing your bank and I ain't about to make a second. We're doing this my way or not at all. I'm taking the girl," the outlaw yelled.

"Promise me that you'll drop her off at the edge of town," Gideon answered back.

"I'll promise you that I'll release her when I get a couple hours away from here as long as you don't follow until then. If I see you coming, she'll be dead," the outlaw yelled.

Gideon's mind raced for an answer on what to do. He could think of no solution that wouldn't get the woman killed. Trying to shoot the outlaw from such a distance with the girl held so closely was too big of a risk. Taking the word of a murdering robber was never a good thing to do either, but he could think of no alternative.

"We'll do it, but you better not harm her or I swear I'll hunt you into the bowels of hell if necessary and kill you," Gideon yelled.

"She'll be fine. Now tell your men," the outlaw yelled.

"Finnie, can you hear me?" Gideon bellowed.

"Aye," Finnie answered.

"You and Blackie throw your guns into the street. We're letting them go. I don't want anybody else killed," Gideon hollered.

Finnie threw his revolver and rifle into the street and retrieved Blackie's shotgun before doing the same with it. "It's done," he yelled.

The outlaw had emerged far enough onto the sidewalk to see what was happening. He had the young woman's head pulled up to his own so that it forced her to stand on her tiptoes to keep from choking.

"Throw down your guns, Zack," Gideon called out as he threw his own guns out into the street.

After seeing Zack throw down his guns, the two outlaws quickly moved to the horses. The outlaw that did all the talking mounted his horse and yanked Betsy up behind him while the second man retrieved the mounts of his dead partners. Galloping away in a cloud of dust, the two outlaws along with Betsy and the three riderless horses disappeared down the street.

Gideon and Zack recovered their weapons and ran down the street towards the bank.

"Gideon, Blackie got shot," Finnie called out.

"Zack, you check on Mr. Fredrick while I tend to Blackie," Gideon ordered.

"How bad is it?" Gideon asked as he jogged up to Finnie and Blackie.

"I don't know. It's his arm and he's in shock," Finnie answered.

Mary barged out of the saloon and waddled towards the men. Tears streamed down her cheeks by the time that she reached the men. "Are you okay?" she asked Finnie.

Nodding his head, Finnie said, "I'm fine."

Throwing her arms around her husband, Mary buried her head against his neck. "I saw what happened. You scared the hell out of me. I thought sure that you were a dead man," she said between sobs.

"We can talk later. Blackie needs to get to Doc," Finnie said as he patted her back. "But calm down. Everything is fine and I don't want you losing the baby."

Zack joined them. "Mr. Fredrick is dead and so are all three of the outlaws," he said.

Gideon and Finnie helped Blackie to his feet and began walking him down the street with Zack and Mary following them.

"Just another quiet day in Last Stand," Gideon said shaking his head.

Chapter 8

The group of five barged into the doctor's office and led Blackie to the exam table. Doc had already begun preparations for treating the wounded after hearing all of the shooting and had laid out his medical instruments.

"Anybody that isn't shot nor has some other malady needs to get out of here. This isn't a saloon," Doc barked.

Finnie and Zack helped Blackie up onto the table. The blacksmith's eyes still looked glassy and when he spoke, his voice had a dreamy sound to it.

"Doc, Blackie is in shock. I've seen it in the war," Finnie said.

Doc looked at Finnie and contemplated asking the Irishman if he wanted to treat the patient, but decided to be nice instead and hold his tongue.

"Would someone find John and his family and ask Henry if he would like to assist me? The boy seems to have some interest in medicine and there's nothing like blood and bullet holes to help decide if doctoring is your calling or not," Doc said.

Gideon began ushering the crowd from the room. "Finnie, go spend some time with Mary before we have to leave. I'm going to keep my word and give them two hours. They can see for miles from some of these ridgetops and I don't want to get Betsy killed by leaving early and getting spotted. Zack and I will take care of the bodies and find Henry," he said.

John and his family were found huddled in their hotel room. They had viewed the carnage in the street from their window. Kate and Rose still trembled from all the gunfire. Henry became excited at the invitation from his grandfather and had to plead his case against his mother's objections for leaving the safety of their room. She finally relented on the condition that John would accompany his son to the doctor's office.

Doc Abram gave Blackie a couple of spoonfuls of laudanum and cut the sleeve of his shirt away. Blackie had managed to recount the details of the robbery with Doc's questioning. As Doc waited for the drug to take effect on his patient, John and Henry walked into the office.

"I had to come with Henry to get Kate to allow him out of the hotel. She's ready to catch the first stagecoach out of here after what we saw," John said as way of explanation for his presence.

"I'd imagine so. Before now, we've never had a bank robbery," Doc noted.

"I'm beginning to think I'm bad luck for your town," John said.

"Henry, I want you to go to the washstand and scrub your hands the cleanest they've ever been," Doc ordered.

After Henry finished washing his hands, Doc poured carbolic acid over them.

"What is that?" Henry asked.

"Carbolic acid helps prevent infections. Normally, I would give my patient chloroform to put them under, but Blackie is in too much shock so I gave him laudanum. It will relax him and he won't remember the pain," Doc said.

Blackie had fallen asleep. Doc poured carbolic acid into the wound entrance before inserting his finger into the hole to probe the wound. The blacksmith moaned, but offered no resistance as the doctor worked.

"The humerus bone has a chip out of it from the bullet, but nothing bad. If the bone were shattered, we'd have real problems. A one-armed blacksmith isn't much use. Do you want to feel it?" Doc said.

The boy looked at the wound and took a breath as he tried to decide whether to put his finger in the hole. "Sure," he finally said.

Henry inserted his finger into the wound, and with Doc's guidance, he probed the wound.

"Do you feel the bone?" Doc asked.

"I do," Henry said excitedly. "I can feel where the bullet took a piece out."

"Okay, now I want you to pour the acid on each instrument that I ask you to hand me. I need those forceps right there," Doc said and pointed.

Doing as instructed, Henry doused the forceps and handed them to his grandfather. The doctor began extracting bits of bone, causing Blackie to moan and put up a small amount of resistance. Henry grabbed the blacksmith's arm without prompting and held it in place until Doc was satisfied that he had gotten all of the chips.

Doc grabbed the sleeve he had cut from the shirt and stretched it out on the countertop. "I want to show you something. Blackie's shirt looks about worn out and the bullet tore the fabric. A lot of times the bullet will take a piece of material into the wound and if you don't retrieve it, the patient will almost always get an infection. Many times they will even die. Now I want you to hold his arm up while I treat the exit wound," he said.

John watched the proceedings with mixed emotions. His son looked as enthused as he had ever seen him and he felt happy for him, but realized that Henry probably wouldn't follow him into the banking business. "Father, you are going to cause me to have to make Rose the next banker in the family," he said.

Doc looked over at his son and smiled. "That would be okay. She strikes me as a smart one and there's nothing wrong with a smart woman. I just wanted to expose Henry to what medicine is really like. Back in medical school, I saw more than one student decide medicine was not their calling the first time they got blood on their hands. Better to know now than after all that schooling," he said.

Henry held the arm in the air while Doc trimmed away the dead skin and doused the back side of the wound with the carbolic acid. The doctor then dressed the wound before declaring the procedure complete.

"Do you think Blackie will be okay?" Henry asked.

"I think so. I'll have to watch for infection. He has a good deal of muscle damage and that will take a couple of months to heal, but he's strong as an ox and I expect a full recovery," Doc answered.

Gideon walked in the office as they were cleaning up the medical instruments. "How is Blackie?" he asked.

"He won't be shoeing any horses anytime soon, but I think he'll be fine," Doc said.

"Good, I'm glad to hear it. Finnie and I are going to have to ride out. Do you think Mary will be fine while he's gone?" Gideon asked.

"Mary is going to be fine as long as she follows my orders and she has so far," Doc said.

"Was Blackie able to tell you what happened?" Gideon asked.

"He did. Sounds like you had a real mess on your hands," Doc said.

"Do you think I did the right thing in letting them take Betsy?" Gideon questioned.

"Gideon, I totally trust your judgement as a sheriff. I know you did what you thought best," Doc answered.

"I'm questioning myself and wondering if I would have done things differently if it would've been Joann. They'd already killed Mr. Fredrick and I think they would've killed Betsy without a thought and then shot it out with us," Gideon said.

"Sounds like you have your answer. Did you talk to Betsy's parents," Doc said.

"I did. Of course they're sick with worry," Gideon said.

"Best thing you can do is get her back. Do you know who you're looking for?" Doc asked.

"I think it's Charlie Reilly. I had a poster for one of the dead outlaws and he's been known to ride with Reilly. That's all I got to go on," Gideon answered.

"Just be careful," Doc reminded him.

Gideon nodded his head before smiling and turning to Henry. "If you decide to follow in your grandad's footsteps, don't be a grouch like he is. His bedside manners leave a lot to be desired," he said.

"Get out of here and go catch the outlaws. Next time I work on you I'm liable to make you a steer," Doc grumbled.

Finnie and Zack waited for Gideon at the jail. Zack would ride with them until they found Betsy and then return her to Last Stand on an extra horse they would take. They followed the tracks west. A mile out of town they found where the outlaws had stopped and switched Betsy to her own horse before resuming their getaway.

"Looks like we're headed back to South Fork," Finnie remarked.

"I doubt these two will stop in at the trading post, but maybe they'll leave Betsy there," Gideon said.

About a mile before reaching the trading post, the tracks of the outlaws stopped again. They had led their horses into the brush and back out again before riding away.

"Maybe Betsy is back in here," Gideon said as he led the way off the road.

Thirty yards into the brush, Gideon found Betsy's dress torn to pieces and thrown into a heap. Gideon could feel his legs go limber and he shuddered as if he caught a chill. The nagging doubt he had since letting the outlaws ride away with Betsy was replaced by dread for what he would see on the other side of a crop of rocks. He walked around the rocks and saw Betsy. She lay stretched out naked on the ground with her throat slit from ear to ear. Her eyes stared up at the heavens and a huge pool of blood surrounded her head.

Finnie and Zack walked up beside Gideon. Zack took one look and dropped to his knees. He puked until his stomach emptied and continued retching dry heaves. Gideon glanced over at Finnie, but neither man spoke. Zack finally stood up and walked away without making eye contact with his friends. He looked as pale as a ghost.

In a voice filled with rage, Gideon said, "I knew I should've never let them leave with Betsy. I could feel it deep inside and I didn't listen to my intuition."

"Gideon, I don't know what we could've done differently. I certainly didn't have a shot and you couldn't of either. We would've got her killed," Finnie said.

"Anything would have been better than this. What would I have done if it would've been Joann?" Gideon asked.

"I don't know, but you did what you thought would give her the best chance to live," Finnie said.

"A lot of good that did. Can you imagine the fear that poor girl felt before she died? We've both been in some tight spots, but I guarantee you that we've never felt fear like she did," Gideon said.

"I know," Finnie said quietly.

Zack rejoined them but made a point of turning his back to the body. "I don't even want to think about how Joann is going to take this. She and Betsy were becoming pretty good friends. This is just terrible. Terrible," he said.

Trying to steer the conversation in another direction, Finnie asked, "Zack, do you have your slicker with you?"

"Yeah, sure. I'll go get it," Zack said.

"I'll buy you a new one out of my expenses," Gideon said as Zack went to retrieve the coat.

Zack returned with the slicker and handed it to Gideon. "I can't help you put it on her. I just can't," he said.

"That's all right. Finnie and I will do it. When you get back to town, I want you to go in on the back street to the cabinetmaker's shop. I don't want anybody seeing Betsey this way," Gideon said.

"I going to have to tell her parents, aren't I?" Zack asked.

Gideon looked at the ground and kicked a pebble. "I'd appreciate it," he said.

After getting the body into the slicker, Gideon and Finnie carried Betsy to the extra horse and tied her across the saddle.

"I hope I never have to do this again," Finnie said.

"I don't care if we have to ride to hell and back, but we're going to find those sons of bitches. I'm going to tie them to a tree and slice their sacks open and cut one nut off at a time and then I'm going to cut off their peckers," Gideon yelled.

"Gideon, you promised Doc that you would never take revenge on an outlaw again, but only bring them to justice," Finnie reminded the sheriff.

Gideon stared Finnie in the eyes. "How did you even know about that? All that happened before you even got here," he said angrily.

In the past, Gideon had intentionally shot a man in the stomach to extract a slow death and had shot another man in the groin. His behavior had nearly fractured his and Doc's relationship until Doc had made him promise never to do such a thing again.

"Doc told me what you did to Hank Sligo and Ted McClean. He also told me that you promised to never do anything like that again," Finnie said.

Gideon continued staring at Finnie before turning his head and spitting on the ground.

Chapter 9

Two days after Zack returned with Betsy's body, Joann remained so despondent over her friend's death that she barely got out of bed. Zack found himself powerless to rally her spirits. In truth, he was struggling with his own shaken emotional state after seeing the gruesome murder scene and could provide little comfort. His growing concern for Joann led him to summon Abby to talk to her daughter. While Abby was there with Winnie and Chance trying to lift her daughter's spirits, Joann's water broke.

"Abs, what's happening?" Joann asked, looking down at the fluid on the floor in surprise. "Aren't I supposed to have contractions before my water breaks?"

"Usually, but it doesn't always happen that way," Abby answered.

"Do you think there's something wrong with the baby?" Joann asked.

"No, I don't think there is anything wrong with the baby. Just relax. I'm sure your contractions will start shortly," Abby said.

"But I'm not ready for the baby. I'm not due for two weeks," Joann protested.

"Well, apparently your baby has other ideas," Abby said. "I'm not really ready to admit that I'm going to be a grandma either, but here we are."

Zack paced around the room. Winnie and Chance stood transfixed as they watched their brother-in-law stride across the room like a bull gone mad.

"What do you want me to do?" Zack asked.

"First things are you need to quit pacing and take a breath. Next, you need to ride to town and tell Doc what happened. I'm sure he'll come directly. Now scoot," Abby said.

By the time Zack returned from town, Joann's contractions caused her to grimace in pain and occasionally let out a moan. Chance wouldn't stop crying as he watched his sister's discomfort. Abby had repeatedly sent the children outside to play, but Winnie's curiosity would quickly lead them back into the cabin where their mother remained too preoccupied to take the time to lay the law down and put a stop to it.

"Doc will be here when he finishes up with his patients. He grumbled about missing a planned dinner with his family this evening," Zack said.

"He'll get over it," Abby said.

"How are you feeling, Joann?" Zack asked.

"How do you think I'm feeling? It hurts," Joann shot back.

"Zack, I need you to take Winnie and Chance to Sarah. I can't watch them and be here for Joann too," Abby said.

"You want me to just drop in and leave the children with her?" Zack asked with misgivings in his voice.

"Yes, Sarah won't mind. We've already talked about it," Abby said.

"Will I miss the baby being born?" he asked.

"No, I don't think your baby is in any hurry to make an appearance. The sooner you leave, the sooner you'll get back," Abby said in an attempt to hurry him.

Winnie nearly had to be dragged from the cabin. She protested all the way to the wagon until Abby grew stern with her daughter as she lifted her into the seat. As a peace offering, Abby promised that she could stay for Joann's next baby.

Zack looked down from the wagon in bewilderment at Abby. "I hope she waits awhile before the next one," he said.

"Well, I'm pretty sure you know how to keep that from happening. What's it worth to you?" Abby said with a devilish grin.

Zack tapped the reins against the horse's rump and took off without answering.

Doc Abram arrived a short time later and walked into the cabin unannounced. He dropped his hat onto the table and looked at the two women with an irritated expression.

"You were supposed to wait until my family headed back east," Doc grumbled.

"Believe me, I would have. The baby didn't get the news," Joann said just before another contraction.

"I know," Doc said. "How far apart are they?"

"Five minutes," Abby answered.

"Let's get you into bed," Doc said and helped Joann to her feet.

Zack returned from delivering the children to Sarah and rushed into the house expecting to have missed out on the baby's arrival. The contractions had not quickened and had even stalled a couple of times. Abby concluded that they were in for a long night and started cooking supper.

Doc walked to the table and sat down, leaving Joann to rest in the bedroom after her contractions had stopped once again. "The first child always likes to take their sweet time coming into the world," he said as he watched Zack pacing.

"Do you think everything is alright?" Zack asked as he stopped and turned towards the doctor.

"Everything is fine except for that damn pacing. Now sit down and eat. You're not pretty enough to keep my interest a strutting back and forth," Doc said.

Zack managed to quell his worrying long enough to smile. He walked over and sat down across from Doc. "I'm sorry we kept you from your dinner," he said.

"That's okay. Abby is a better cook anyways," Doc said.

"I'm surprised you didn't make Zack go get Sarah. I know what you all think about her cooking," Abby said as she brought the beefsteaks to the table.

Doc grinned. "You never heard me say that," he said.

"Uh-huh. Not to my face anyways," Abby said.

"Have you gotten a telegram from Gideon?" Doc asked to change the subject.

"No, not a word. He has me worried. Zack said that he and Finnie got into it over Gideon's plans when he catches the men and a promise he made to you," Abby said as she sat down at the table.

"He was just blowing off steam. He'll do the right thing. Gideon is a man of his word," Doc assured her before cutting a bite of steak.

"I hope you're right. I know he's got to be blaming himself for Betsy's death," Abby said.

They ate the rest of the meal in silence, each too preoccupied with the coming birth to make conversation. Just as they finished the meal, Joann let out a wail.

"Sounds like it's time for us to get back to work," Abby said and headed to the bedroom, leaving the dishes on the table.

"Abs, how did you ever do this three times?" Joann cried out as her mother entered the room.

"You'll forget all about the pain when you hold that baby," Abby answered.

"I wish Momma and Poppa were here. I know they feel left out since I moved down here with you. I want my momma," Joann said.

"I know," Abby said. She felt surprised by her own lack of jealousy that Joann wanted the woman that raised her by her side. "They need to come for a visit. I wrote Aunt Rita last week and told her as much."

"And Daddy is missing out too," Joann said as Doc entered the room.

"You'll have a big surprise for Gideon when he gets back," Abby assured her.

Doc checked Joann's progress before declaring, "The baby is on the way."

A hard contraction caused Joann to scream. "Zackary Barlow is never touching me again," she swore.

Just after midnight, Joann gave one final push and the baby slid out into the world. Joann closed her eyes and fell back in exhaustion. Doc quickly cut the umbilical cord before holding the newborn upside down and delivering a sound smack. The air crackled with the cry of the baby taking her first breath.

"You have a healthy little girl," Doc announced.

Abby took the baby and began cleaning the newborn. Her eyes welled up with tears as she wrapped her granddaughter in a blanket. Life had taken so many twists and turns in the last few years that the moment overwhelmed her. She took one more look at the baby before presenting the child to its mother. The baby had some blond fuzz on her head and about the prettiest face Abby had ever seen. "She's beautiful and she has your and Gideon's pretty blue eyes," she said.

"She is beautiful," Joann said as she looked down at her daughter and nestled her.

"I'll go get Zack. I need to sit down and rest," Doc said as he shuffled out the door.

Zack rushed into the room. He looked dark under the eyes and had paced himself to near exhaustion. A smile came upon his face and he stood at the foot of the bed as if afraid to come any closer.

"Come here and see your daughter," Joann coaxed.

He stepped nearer and ran his finger down the babies face. "She looks like you. We really have a baby," Zack said in astonishment.

"Do you want to hold her?" Joann asked.

"I don't know how. Maybe I should wait awhile," Zack said.

Without prompting, Abby took the baby and placed her in Zack's arms. He held the baby next to his large frame as if she might break or be snatched away by wolves.

"Tess Ann Barlow, I'm your daddy," Zack said.

Chapter 10

The sign read Junction City. Gideon had never been this far west in the New Mexico Territory and knew nothing of the area. They had tracked the outlaws for three days with no sign that they were gaining ground on them. In fact, Gideon feared that the killers had actually gained distance with their ability to switch between horses to keep their mounts fresh.

Sizing up the place, Gideon decided that Junction City didn't look like much of a town as he and Finnie rode into the village in the afternoon. A saloon, hotel, and a couple of stores made up the main street. Two men walked down the boardwalk, but nothing else stirred in the town.

He and Finnie tied their horses in front of the saloon and walked through the door. The place looked cleaner than most saloons Gideon had frequented in the past and didn't reek of smoke and stale beer. A bartender stood ready to serve and four customers lounged at the bar not paying any attention to the new arrivals.

"I recognize two of those men. They used to be miners at Animas City," Finnie said as they stood at the entrance and looked around the saloon.

"Were you on good terms with them?" Gideon asked.

"Sure. Good enough," Finnie answered.

"See what they know," Gideon said.

Finnie walked up to the two men. "Hey, boys, it's been awhile. How are you doing?" he asked.

The two men turned and studied Finnie.

"Well, if it isn't Finnie Ford. Look at you. You've gone from Animas City's town drunk to a deputy. You're moving up in the world. The Red Eye Saloon about went under from the loss of your business," the nearest man said with sarcasm dripping from his voice.

"Yeah, Homer, I've cleaned myself up. The sheriff and I are tracking a couple of men that raped and slit the throat of a young woman. We know they came through here and we were hoping somebody could provide us some information about them," Finnie said.

"Well, at least she got a good screwing before she died," Homer said and laughed.

Gideon watch as the bartender and the other three men averted their eyes from the conversation. They appeared to want no part of the exchange. Gideon moved his hand to his revolver. He seethed below the surface and rubbed his fingers together in agitation, but betrayed no expression on his face. The miner would get one more chance to answer the question.

"Homer, there's no call to talk like that. She was a fine girl," Finnie said.

"Go to hell, you little drunk," Homer said.

Gideon drew his Colt and slammed it upside Homer's head so quickly that the man never had a chance to flinch before being knocked silly. As Homer dropped to the floor, Gideon cocked his revolver and pressed it against the temple of the other miner that Finnie knew.

"I don't give a damn which one of you talks, but somebody is going to tell us what we want to know or there won't be a one of you standing when we're through," Gideon warned.

The bartender turned towards Gideon. "I'll help you. Just calm down. Homer likes to run his mouth after he drinks a couple of whiskeys. The two men were in here. They rode in this morning and had baths and breakfast at the hotel. Later on, they came in here and had a drink before leaving maybe three hours ago. I recognized one of them as Charlie Reilly. He called the other one Sal. They were talking about Mexico," he said.

"Thank you. Give us two beers, please," Gideon said.

"Don't you think we need to go?" Finnie asked.

"One beer won't change much," Gideon said. "We'll get them."

Gideon tipped the bartender generously and talked with him as they sipped their beers. By the time they had nearly finished their brews, Homer was sitting up but still on the floor. All the fight had been knocked out of him and he did not speak, but continued to rub his head. Gideon tipped his mug towards Homer as if toasting the former miner and then drank his last swallow.

Outside of the saloon, Gideon said, "We need to get some supplies. This might take some time before we catch them."

After purchasing salt pork, jerky, and hardtack, they picked up the trail outside of the town.

"Don't you find it odd that they took the time for baths and such? I wonder if they think we've given up on catching them," Finnie said.

"I thought of that too. Maybe this is all a game to Charlie and that is his way of taunting us," Gideon said.

"Could turn out to be a deadly game he's playing," Finnie said.

"Oh, it's going to be deadly alright. I guess your old miner friends don't remember you as fondly as you thought," Gideon teased, wanting to change the subject.

"Apparently not. I was a happy drunk. Seems like old Homer just had a hair up his ass," Finnie said.

"And a lump up side his head," Gideon said.

"You could be a granddaddy by now," Finnie said.

"No, Joann wouldn't do that. She'll wait until I get back," Gideon said.

"Well, listen to you. I guess the world stops for the convenience of Gideon Johann. I think the baby might have more to say about the matter than Joann does. And your grandbaby might not be all that impressed with the legend of Gideon Johann. She might just think you're the sweet old guy that spoils her," Finnie said.

Gideon grinned at Finnie. "Could be. I kind of wish it would be a girl, but I'm just sure it's a boy," he said.

"You can be an unbearable man. You don't know whether it's a boy or girl any more than I do. You have half a chance of being right," Finnie said.

After riding for a few minutes, Gideon remarked, "It's a long ways to Mexico."

"Well, let's hope we catch them before they get that far. I have no desire to sit on a horse all the way down there," Finnie said.

They rode for a couple of hours without much conversation. The farther they traveled the more brown and barren the land became. Hills dotted the landscape that looked as bare as a baby's butt. The air heated up and the horses were in a lather by the time they came upon a small creek.

"They're riding straight southwest. We'll rest the horses and continue after dark. I'm going to find those bastards," Gideon said.

"I hope you're right. This place has to be what hell looks like," Finnie said as he bent over to fill his canteen.

Chapter 11

Sunlight had barely found its way to the streets of Last Stand when Blackie entered the doctor's office. Doc stood at the stove staring impatiently at the coffee pot as if he could will the water to boil. He turned his head to see the source of the sound of the door shutting.

"Blackie, you're mighty early. Is something wrong?" Doc asked.

"I don't consider myself a sissy, but my arm hurts. I didn't get any sleep last night," Blackie said.

"Did you take the two spoonfuls of laudanum before bed like I prescribed?" Doc inquired.

"No, sir. I've heard tales of people getting addicted to that stuff and turning crazy like a rabid dog," Blackie said.

"Good God, Blackie. Don't you think I know what I'm doing? As long as you stick to what I prescribed, you'll be fine. You need your rest for your arm to heal properly. That bone injury will cause deep pain. Now sit down and let me have a look," Doc admonished.

"Okay, okay, I'll try it tonight," Blackie said as he hopped up onto the table.

Doc removed the bandage and examined the wound. The tissue looked nice and pink and had begun to heal. "The arm looks good. Just keep using it as much as possible without overdoing things," he said as he retrieved a new bandage.

"Do you think I could use my arm for holding tongs so I could hammer?" Blackie asked.

"I'd wait a couple more days. All that jarring may tear things open," Doc answered.

"Are you ready for me to hitch up the buckboard?" Blackie asked as he stood.

"Yes, I'll come with you in case you need some help," Doc said.

"I can't imagine those city folks riding in a buckboard. Does your family know what you have in store for them?" Blackie asked.

"Not yet. The kids will think it's an adventure. We'll have fun," Doc said as he followed the blacksmith out the door.

After helping Blackie hitch the horses, Doc took the wagon to the feed store and borrowed some sacks of feed for the children to sit on. By the time he pulled the wagon up in front of his office, John and his family stood on the sidewalk waiting for him. To his surprise, all of the family except for Kate dressed in trousers and work shirts. They could have passed for any of the ranch families in Last Stand.

"You'll all be wearing spurs before you know it," Doc said as the family climbed into the wagon.

They rode a mile west out of town to where the vistas came into view. John excitedly pointed out the mountain ranges and the children stood up in the back of the wagon, enthralled with the landscape. Doc noticed that Kate sat unusually silent.

"Kate, you're awfully quiet. Don't you enjoy the scenery?" Doc asked.

"To tell you the truth, Doc, I'm kind of nervous. Between John getting shot and the bank robbery, it makes me think that somebody is liable to jump out of nowhere and shoot us. And Gideon and Finnie being gone and leaving no law around bothers me too," Kate said.

"Sometimes bad things do happen out here, but bad things happen back in Boston all the time too. It's just that Boston is so big that it doesn't seem as personal as it does in a little town. There are a lot of things about Last Stand that are much safer than where you live. You can walk anywhere in town and not worry about getting mugged or pickpocketed and the people are pretty darned friendly too," Doc said.

Kate smiled for the first time since leaving town. "I suppose you are correct," she said.

"Of course, I'm right," Doc said with a chuckle. "Wisdom is old age's saving grace. Now enjoy this land. This is God's country."

Doc followed the roads that worked their way in an arc to the north. They traveled at a leisurely pace, stopping often to view the mountains or a stream with water so blue as to amaze the children. John spied five elk sunning on a mountainside. He patiently had to point them out until each member of his family finally spotted the animals. As the road curved back to the southeast, Zack and Joann's cabin came into view.

Arrangements had already been made for Doc to make a call on the new baby. With Joann's blessing, Sarah and Abby had conspired to prepare a feast of elk meat for John. He had been promised the meal on his previous visit, but the dinner had never come to fruition. When the family pulled up to the Barlow homestead, both Sarah and Abby's buckboards were out front. Ethan, Zack, and Benjamin sat on the front porch.

"Looks like there's a crowd," Kate noted.

"Everybody is excited to meet you and your family," Doc said as he climbed down from the wagon and retrieved his doctor's bag.

Ethan and Zack walked down the steps and shook John's hand. John introduced his family before Zack ushered them into the cabin where introductions were again made. Sarah and Abby cooked while Joann walked the fussy baby. Tess had spent most of the night crying and Joann looked exhausted and at her wits' end. Kate gladly relieved the young mother of her child and began walking the room.

"I can never get enough of babies. Fussy or not, I love holding them," Kate said.

Joann sat down in a chair and looked as if she melted into her seat. "I'm so tired," she said.

"You don't need all this company. We shouldn't stay," Kate said.

Sarah turned from the stove. "Doc and I promised John a home-cooked elk steak and the meal will be ready shortly. Joann could use the support," she said.

Abby pulled Doc aside in a corner.

"Joann's milk hasn't come in good. Tess wasn't getting enough to eat so I've been bringing cow milk. I think it's made her colicky," Abby told the doctor.

"I plan to have a look at her and Joann," Doc said.

"I need to go help Sarah," Abby said.

Doc took the baby from Kate and motioned for Joann to follow him to the bedroom. He laid the baby on the bed and began examining her.

"So how are you feeling?" he asked Joann.

"I'm tired. We haven't gotten much sleep around here the last couple of days. Tess has me worried.

What if my milk doesn't come in and she can't take cow's milk?" she asked.

"Your milk will come. The baby came early ahead of her food supply. Zack will just have to get a goat. Their milk is easier on babies," Doc said.

"Do you think she's alright?" Joann asked.

"She's colicky for sure and on the thin side, but I think she'll be fine. We'll put that husband of yours to work after we eat and I expect in a couple more days you'll be supplying all the milk the baby could want," Doc said.

Doc listened to the baby's heart and pronounced it strong. He then examined Joann and questioned her more about her condition since the birth.

"I'm just tired from lack of sleep. I can cry at the drop of a hat and I'm so worried that Tess isn't getting enough to eat. I'm afraid she'll be stunted," Joann confessed.

"She'd have to get so much skinner than she is to stunt her growth. Quit wasting your time thinking about that. We won't let it happen. You need to try to get your rest. Your body is going through a lot of changes and first time mothers worry too much. Everything will be fine. I promise," Doc assured her.

Satisfied with both exams, Doc escorted Joann and Tess to the front of the house.

"You're right on time," Sarah announced.

Ethan gave the blessing. The children sat on the floor and the adults crowded around the table. Kate warily examined the meat on her plate, trying her best to conceal her doubts about eating wild meat. She watched as her husband grabbed his fork and knife and attacked the steak with gusto.

"This is way better than the elk I had at the hotel. Sarah and Abby, you did a fine job," John proclaimed.

Kate took her first tentative bite. She chewed the meat methodically as she judged the taste. To her surprise, the meat tasted a lot like beef but a little sweeter. The wild gamey taste that she had always heard others talk about was not present. She smiled at Sarah and Abby. "You two might make ranchers out of us yet," she said.

For the rest of the meal, the conversations bounced between life out west and in Boston. Any reservations Kate felt about fitting in with the rancher wives soon faded from her memory as she found herself engaged in conversations as if she had known them all her life. Even Joann, at her young age, had a spirit and feistiness that Kate found admirable.

As they finished the meal, Doc said, "Zack, you need to head to the Kramer homestead and see if Pell will sell or let you borrow a goat. Tess needs goat milk."

Zack looked around the room and found everybody looking back at him. Doc's orders had caught the new father off-guard and he felt like a boy again. He noticed Henry sitting on the floor with the children. The young man didn't fit in with the young ones and the table had been too crowded to sit with the adults. "Henry, I can saddle two horses if you would like to ride with me," he said.

"Really?" Henry said.

"Sure," Zack answered.

"But I've never ridden a horse," Henry said.

"The worst thing that can happen is that you break your neck and your grandpa can fix just about anything. And if he can't fix it, I'm sure he can at least boss you around and tell you what you need to do," Zack said and grinned at the doctor.

John said, "Go with him. It'll be a good experience for you."

Henry followed Zack out of the cabin and watched as the horses were saddled. Zack gave him a brief lesson on riding and showed him how to use the reins properly. The young man swung himself into the saddle as if he had been riding his whole life, but then froze as the horse started walking.

"What do I do? What do I do?" Henry asked nervously.

"Pull the reins back lightly and say whoa. Just relax. That's a gentle horse. He's not going to hurt you," Zack told him.

Riding in the yard, Henry worked with the horse until he felt confident that he could control the animal. The longer he rode the more his stiff posture began to relax. He finally smiled and said, "Let's go. I think I got the hang of it."

By the time the two men rode away, the other adults had enough of kids in the house. Benjamin, Winnie, Rose, and Tad were ordered outdoors, leaving Chance crying for his sister.

As they walked out the door, Ethan said, "Benjamin, make sure to keep Tad away from the well. He's not old enough to know better."

Winnie was enthralled with Rose. Doc's granddaughter was just enough older, and with her Boston accent and citified ways, she seemed worldly to Winnie. Even more exciting was the fact that Rose seemed to really like her too. The two walked around the homestead talking like long lost friends while Benjamin followed and kept an eye on Tad.

They made their way to the stream where the water pooled. Winnie taught Rose how to skip flat rocks across the water. Benjamin joined the competition to see who could skip a rock the farthest.

Tad played along the water's edge and stepped on an algae covered rock. The slick slime caused his feet to slip out from under him and he fell head first into the pool. The water was over his head and he went completely under the surface.

Benjamin yanked his boots off and dove into the water. The clear water made spotting the child easy. He grabbed Tad under the arms and shot to the surface. The little boy coughed and cried all at the same time and acted hysterical. Benjamin recollected doing nearly the exact same thing when he was about Tad's age. His father had dove in and instead of rushing out of the water or getting mad, he had played in the water with Benjamin until the fear disappeared.

"Tad, you're okay. Look, this is fun," Benjamin soothed as he started walking the child around in the pool.

The child quit crying, but continued to wrap his arms around Benjamin's neck in a death grip.

Winnie and Rose watched the rescue with admiration. Winnie already knew that she would marry Benjamin someday and she swelled with pride at his bravery. She also desperately wanted to get in the water too.

"Let's get in with them. We can say we were helping to show Tad that there is nothing to be scared about," Winnie said.

"Won't your mom be mad?" Rose asked.

"Probably," Winnie said as she took off her shoes. "The worst she will do is yell and maybe spank me. It won't be the first time and it probably won't be the last."

Winnie did a cannonball into the water. Rose watched reluctantly from the bank until the pull of fitting in got the best of her and she removed her shoes. She walked into the water gingerly, gasping at the chill of the water. The two girls began splashing each other and Tad laughed as he watched the water fight. He started to relax his grip on Benjamin until the older boy was able to hold him out and let the child splash at the girls.

After Joann, Chance, and Tess had all fallen asleep, the others walked outdoors with the intent to sit on the porch. They heard all the giggles down by the stream and decided they best go investigate. There they found the four children still playing in the water.

"Gwendolyn Hanson, what in tarnation is going on here?" Abby hollered out before anyone else had the chance.

"Tad fell in the water and Benjamin rescued him. He's a hero. Rose and I had to get into the water and show Tad that it was fun so he wouldn't be scared anymore. He was really scared," Winnie answered.

Abby folded her arms and pretended to glare at Winnie. She knew her daughter had bested her. Her inclination was to grin at Winnie's fierce independence, but she didn't dare. Winnie did not need any encouragement.

"I bet you did. I just bet you did," Abby said.

Chapter 12

Riding into the night to catch the outlaws had proved fruitless. Gideon and Finnie had ridden to nearly midnight before stopping when they feared they had wandered off course and lost the track. That night they went to sleep too tired to eat and feeling dejected. The next morning they were relieved to find that they were still on the correct course.

Three days later, they still had not caught up with the fugitives and no matter how hard they pushed, they would always find that the outlaws had camped two to three hours ahead of them. The horses looked worn down and thin from all the travel. The land was barren of vegetation except when they came upon water, forcing them to spend extra time there to allow the animals to graze.

The two lawmen were tired and dirty. Their body odor became seared into their nostrils. They would ride for hours without saying a word. Every subject that they usually debated, they had talked to death. Wondering aloud about the conditions of Joann and Mary were about the only things they bothered discussing.

"Gideon, we're going to ride the horses into the ground if we go much farther," Finnie said.

"I know. I hope we come upon some water. We'll rest and then try riding into the night one more time. If we fail again, we'll go home. I should have planned this better and brought extra mounts. This failure is all on me," Gideon said.

"We underestimated them for sure. I still can't believe they haven't slowed down their pace. They must feel certain we're still on their trail," Finnie said.

"I wish I knew this area. If we could find a town, I'd buy some fresh horses, but I don't know where the hell we are," Gideon said.

"I think we've died and gone to hell," Finnie lamented.

In mid-afternoon, they came upon a canyon. Looking down into valley, they could see a little lake and the greenest landscape that they'd seen in days.

"Do you think it's a mirage?" Finnie joked.

"No, I think it's Eden. Maybe Charlie and Sal will be down there with their hands in the air waiting for us to arrest them," Gideon said.

They rode down the steep trail to the bottom where they unsaddled the horse and turned them loose. They found the remains of a campfire that the outlaws had kicked into oblivion before moving on, leaving no way to determine if they had left the spot an hour or many hours ago. Gideon retrieved a bar of soap from his saddlebag and began shedding clothes. He marched into the water while Finnie still studied their surroundings.

"Good God, your ass is white. It shines like the sun. I think you've blinded me," Finnie said.

"I wouldn't admit that I looked at it if I were you. Maybe I don't know you as well as I thought," Gideon said.

"Aren't you worried about Indians? I'd think this would be a prime spot to cross paths with some," Finnie said.

"I probably should be. If you see any, I'll shine my ass and blind them while you shoot them," Gideon said.

Finnie waited until Gideon dressed before he bathed. He remained nervous about Indians and kept his eyes on the rim of the canyon as he scrubbed. Gideon stretched out on the ground and snored loudly by the time the Irishman waded out of the water. Looking around one more time, Finnie resigned himself to the fact that he needed a nap more than he feared Indians and fell to sleep.

The sound of Buck nickering woke up both men. They jumped up and realized that the sun had sunk below the rim of the canyon.

"We're lucky we didn't wake up with our scalps on some buck's spear," Finnie said.

"When did you get so scared of Indians? Let's eat and get going. We're going to find Charlie tonight. I can feel it," Gideon said.

Starvation almost seemed preferable to another meal of jerky and hardtack. Gideon wished he could retrieve his bottle of whiskey to wash down the food, but he didn't like drinking in front of Finnie since the Irishman swore off the stuff. He contented himself with fresh water.

"I almost feel alive again," Gideon said as he threw the saddle onto Buck.

"I'll feel alive when we get back home. At the rate we're going, my baby will be born and in school by the time we get there," Finnie said as he mounted his horse.

They rode out of the canyon and back into the same bleak landscape that they had traveled for days. The horses seemed reenergized and picked up their feet instead of tripping on rocks as they had been wont to do earlier in the day. As dusk settled over the land, they were still following the outlaws towards the southwest.

"Are we still planning on riding into the night?" Finnie asked skeptically.

"We are. I promise that if we don't find them, we'll turn back. I've been riding Buck too many years to kill him now. We've pushed them as far as we can," Gideon answered.

Night fell and Gideon and Finnie pushed on. The silence of the land became more pronounced in the dark. The land was too inhospitable for even bugs and the clatter of the horse's hoofs provided the only sound to interrupt the eerie quiet.

As midnight approached, Gideon pulled his horse to a stop at the top of a rise. "Looks like I was wrong again. I've let poor Betsy down in every way imaginable. Sometimes I hate this job. Let's make camp and we'll head home in the morning," he said.

Finnie stared out into the abyss. "Gideon, is that my imagination or is that a speck of light?" he asked.

Gideon squinted his eyes and concentrated on gazing into the darkness. He could feel goosebumps pop up on his arms and the hair on his neck stand on end as he saw the fire. "I could kiss you, you little Irish leprechaun," he said.

"How far away do you think that campfire is?" Finnie asked.

"I don't have a clue, but we're about to find out," Gideon said as he nudged his horse into moving.

They rode for what seemed like miles before the fire in the distance began to appear noticeably larger. Another half-hour past and they were finally getting close.

"How are we going to do this?" Finnie whispered.

"Let's just keep riding nice and easy. If they stir, we'll charge them. We're in the dark and they're in the light," Gideon said.

As they neared within thirty yards, Gideon could see that the outlaws were camped by a little pool of water with some surrounding scrub trees that must have provided the firewood. He could see the two men stretched out on the ground under their bedrolls. One of the fugitive's horses nickered and the men stirred.

"Charlie, something's out there," Sal hollered.

Gideon and Finnie let out screams that sounded like a combination of a Rebel yell and an Indian war whoop and kicked their horses into a gallop. The two outlaws fumbled for their guns and labored out from under their bedrolls. They seemed confused from which direction the riders were advancing and spun one direction and then the other.

Sal fired the first shot as Finnie closed in on him. The shot missed and before the outlaw could shoot again, Finnie aimed his Colt and fired. Sal took a step backwards and collapsed. Gideon ran Charlie over with his horse before the murderer could aim his gun. The force of the collision sent the outlaw airborne and he landed hard on his back. Jerking Buck to a stop, Gideon jumped off his horse and moved towards the outlaw. Charlie had managed to hold onto his gun and he struggled to his feet.

"Drop your gun. It's over," Gideon hollered.

Charlie looked over at Finnie and then at Gideon. He stood unsteadily on his feet and swayed a drunkard.

"And let you take me back to hang? Go to hell," Charlie said and raised his gun.

A barrage of bullets from Gideon and Finnie slammed into Charlie Reilly. Each shot drove him a step backwards and he toppled over never having fired his gun.

Finnie dismounted and moved cautiously to check Sal. "Sal's dead," he called out.

"Charlie's real dead," Gideon announced.

Finnie holstered his revolver and dragged Sal into the darkness. He then helped Gideon drag the much larger Charlie off beside his fallen companion. They then rifled through the saddlebags of the five horses that the robbers had ridden and found bags of gold coins. Gideon and Finnie looked up at each other and smiled with satisfaction before walking back to the fire and plopping down onto the ground.

"We might have some reward money coming," Gideon said.

"Well, we deserve it if we do. I haven't ridden this hard since the war and I was a lot younger back then," Finnie said.

"Thank you for spotting that fire. You know I would've never been at peace going home. Letting them get away would have haunted me forever," Gideon said.

"I know," Finnie replied.

"I hope we get home before those babies are born," Gideon said.

"Gideon, what would you have done to these two if we hadn't killed them?" Finnie asked.

Gideon smiled sadly and let out a sigh. "I was going to keep my word to Doc, but I sure planned to make them think I was about to castrate their good-for-nothing balls," he said.

"Good," Finnie said.

"Yeah, keeping promises can be a challenge," Gideon said wryly.

"Go ahead and have a drink of whiskey. I don't mind. I'd give that stuff up a hundred times over for Mary," Finnie said.

Grinning, Gideon walked over to Buck and grabbed the bottle from his saddlebag. He took a long pull on the bottle before corking it and putting it back.

"Did I ever tell you that you're a pretty good friend when you're not being a blabbering fool?" Gideon asked.

"I guess I'll take that as a compliment. As good as I'll likely ever get from you. What now?" Finnie said.

"I'm ready to sleep," Gideon answered.

"You mean we're going to go to bed with those bodies right over there in the shadows?" Finnie questioned.

"Unless you plan on covering them with rock in the dark by yourself," Gideon said.

"Their ghosts will probably slash our throats in the middle of the night. Our souls will roam in this godforsaken land forever," Finnie lamented.

"And there goes the blabbering fool," Gideon said as he stretched out and closed his eyes.

Chapter 13

Pausing at the turnoff to the side road, Gideon had to decide whether to turn north to go home or continue east with Finnie back to town. He so wanted to go see Abby and get away from Finnie for a while. Finnie had begun worrying about Mary the moment they had headed back home after killing the outlaws. Gideon had listened to the loquacious Irishman repeat the same things over so many times that he thought his brain had gone numb. Deciding that he best ride to town to make sure that it hadn't burned down in their absence, he nudged Buck on.

"I'm about afraid to see what awaits me," Finnie said.

"Finnie, everything is going to be fine when we get there. I just know it. Relax," Gideon said.

The admonishment hurt Finnie's feelings and he hushed, but didn't stop worrying. Nearly losing Mary during her miscarriage had scared him so badly that he never really got over it. Gideon could act all calm now, but Finnie knew that the ordeal shook his friend to the core. In his own way, Gideon needed Mary in his life just as much as Finnie did and the Irishman accepted the unusual relationship. He seldom ever thought about the fact that Gideon and Mary had a brief relationship before Abby came back into Gideon's life. More important things now occupied his mind than what had happened in the past.

Arriving in town just after dark, Gideon and Finnie rode straight to the jail and locked the recovered loot in a cell. Gideon took the key and shoved it into his saddlebag. They then walked all the horses down to the livery stable and beckoned the blacksmith.

Blackie walked out and greeted the sheriff and deputy. The blacksmith had lost some weight since the shooting and he still moved his arm somewhat stiffly. He nonetheless proudly showed off his healing limb. He had been able to resume using the arm for light work and appeared well on his way to making a full recovery.

"These are the outlaws' horses. I need you to put them up until we do something with them," Gideon said.

"Sure. It's good to see you and Finnie made it back," Blackie said.

"I'm just sorry you got shot helping us. I owe you," Gideon said.

"I guess I got a good story out of the deal," Blackie said.

"Make sure you give my horse some extra oats. That poor thing is skin and bones," Finnie said.

"Don't you worry. I'll ease him back up on his rations," Blackie said.

The two lawmen walked across the street to the restaurant that Finnie and Mary had opened. They both were starving and hoping to find Mary and food. She looked up from what had once been the bar and did a double take at the two scroungy looking men standing in the doorway. Letting out a squeal, she waddled to them. In the nearly two weeks that Gideon and Finnie had been gone, Mary's belly had grown considerably.

"My God, I've been worried about you two," Mary said as she hugged Finnie.

"I've nearly drove Gideon crazy fretting over you," Finnie said.

Mary pulled back from Finnie and covered her mouth and nose with her hand. "I love you and I've missed you, but this baby and I can't take those kinds of smells. You two are rank," Mary said and tried to will herself not to gag.

"But Mary, we're starving. We haven't had a real meal since we left here," Finnie protested.

"There's cowboy dirty and then there's you two. You'll have to come in from the alley and sit in that back room. I can't have you in here. You'll run off all our customers. But I promise I'll get you both a big steak," she said.

Gideon grinned at her. "She names a restaurant Mary's Place and starts getting all uppity about her clientele," he said.

"They wouldn't have let you in here back when this was that one-bit saloon and that's saying something," Mary replied.

"Come on, Finnie. The lady is holding all the cards. Let's do what she asks so we can eat," Gideon said.

Gideon and Finnie walked around to the back alley and entered the rear room of the restaurant. Mary joined them, but sat in the corner to avoid the smell.

"How are you feeling?" Finnie asked.

"Good. I'm starting to wear out easier now and the baby kicks the tar out of me, but I'm feeling good. Our baby can come anytime that it wants. That would suit me just fine," Mary said.

"How is Joann feeling?" Gideon asked Mary.

"As far as I know, she's doing well," Mary answered.

"So she hasn't had the baby yet?" Gideon inquired.

Mary opened her mouth to speak and faltered. "You need to go home and let Abby catch you up on the news," she said.

"Damn, I missed the birth of my first grandchild just like I missed out on Joann's birth. History repeating itself. Is it a boy or girl?" Gideon said.

"Gideon, let Abby tell you. She'll want to surprise you," Mary said.

"Mary, I'm dying to know. I'll act surprised when Abby tells me. I know it's a boy anyways," Gideon said.

"Oh, please, you're the worst actor I've ever come across and I've known plenty. I'll just say to not be so sure of yourself," Mary said.

"It's a girl? Hot damn, that's what I hoped she'd have," Gideon said, leaning back in his chair and smiling.

Charlotte entered the room with plates carrying large T-bone steaks, potatoes, and greens. Never known for sugarcoating things, she said, "I've slopped pigs that didn't smell as bad as you two do."

Annoyed, Finnie said, "We'll remember that the next time we face down a bunch of men looking to take you back to Paradise."

Charlotte had run away from a radical religious community to avoid an arranged marriage. Gideon and Finnie had protected and sheltered her during the ordeal.

The girl took particular delight in needling Finnie. "Don't be so harsh. I pray for you and Mary every night that the baby doesn't look like you," Charlotte said before swiftly exiting the room.

While Gideon and Mary laughed, Finnie said, "She's meaner than a bobcat. That fellow that wanted to marry her don't know how lucky he is."

Gideon cut a chunk of steak and forked it into his mouth. The taste of good food made him sigh with pleasure. He concluded that the steak might be the best he'd ever eaten. "Is there any other big news?" he asked.

"I'm not the town crier. Wait until tomorrow before you catch up on everything," Mary said.

"Oh, no. What is it? Tell me or I'll wonder about it all night," Gideon said.

"I've known children that weren't as worrisome as you. Some more cattle were rustled last week. You can't do anything about it now. They're long gone. Eat your steak and go home to Abby. You can worry about things tomorrow," Mary said.

"Thank God we're back. I don't know how Finnie and I would have survived another day without a woman's guidance. By the way, this steak is delicious. You'll probably own the hotel and all the shops in Last Stand before it's all said and done," Gideon said.

Ignoring the jests, Mary asked, "Did you get your men?"

Finnie swallowed his bite of food first and spoke. "We did. We had to chase them through hell, but we got them. All nice and proper too," he said.

"That's good to know. The good doctor had faith that justice would be served as promised. I'm sure Betsy's parents will be grateful," she said.

"Zack has got a big mouth," Gideon said before taking another bite.

"I guess since I already told you about the rustling, I might as well let you know that the town is all riled up about the bank robbery. Anybody with enough money to have a bank account is worried that they've lost all their savings. Some of them are blaming you for Betsy's death too," Mary said.

"I blame me too. I just don't think Betsy had a chance no matter what I would have done. We recovered the money. I guess we got all of it," Gideon said.

"That should help calm things down," Mary said.

"How are the banker's wife and Betsy's parents doing?" Gideon asked.

"Mrs. Fredrick is beside herself. Some of the women in town are taking turns staying with her. The town took up a collection and I heard that the bank gave her some money. Betsy's parents are keeping to themselves. I know that Ethan has been visiting them," Mary answered.

"They both were good people and died way too young," Gideon said.

After finishing the meal, Gideon said goodbye and walked towards Buck. Even in the poor street light, he could see the animal's ribs and that he looked worn down. His horse would need some time to recover.

"One more ride," Gideon said to the horse as he mounted.

Even though he was anxious to get home, Gideon kept the horse in a walk all the way there.

"Abigail Johann, your man is home," Gideon bellowed from the yard.

A moment later, the door opened. Abby with Winnie by her side, bolted outdoors.

"Gideon, we've been so worried about you. I've barely slept this last week. I feared I'd never see you again or know what happened to you," Abby said.

"We had a time of it. You best stay back. Mary and Charlotte informed us in no uncertain terms how bad we smelled. I guess we should have stopped and bathed in the river, but we just wanted to get home," Gideon said.

"Well, come on in then and I'll start heating water. You'll feel better after a good bath anyways. We can get caught up while you wash," Abby said.

Gideon dragged the tub they used for bathing out while Abby began heating water. She sent Winnie to go play in her room when the water was ready. Gideon shed his clothes and threw them out onto the porch before climbing into the tub.

"Oh, this feels so good. Would you please fix me a pipe? I probably need to soak the grime loose anyhow," Gideon said.

Abby made up the pipe and handed it to him. She struck a match and held it above the tobacco as Gideon puffed. Once lit, she retrieved a chair and sat down beside him.

"Well, Grandpa Johann, you have a granddaughter," Abby said.

Gideon let out a war whoop. "That's what I wanted. I just wish I had been here. How are they doing?" he asked, priding himself in the acting job that he had just pulled off. He made a mental note to himself to inform Mary of his thespian skills.

"They're doing well. Zack had to get a goat because Tess wasn't getting enough to eat, but nature has solved all that and she's putting on weight now," Abby said.

"Tess, huh? I like the name. We'll have to ride over to see them in the morning," he said.

"She's a little doll baby," she gushed.

"How's Chance?" he asked.

"Good. He's missed you. I thought I was never going to get him down tonight. He kept saying Daddy," Abby said.

Grinning, Gideon said, "That's my boy."

"Gideon, I want another baby," Abby said.

"We could try here in a little while," Gideon said optimistically.

"I'm not sure I want one that badly. You may need two baths before I let you touch me," Abby teased. "I missed you so much. You can't be gone that long again."

Chapter 14

Gideon rode to town from Joann's cabin in a state of jubilation. He had ridden Abby's horse over to see his new granddaughter and Abby had followed on the buckboard with the children. Holding Tess for the first time might not have been as monumental as embracing Chance on the day he'd been born, but it made for a close second. Visions of someday taking Tess and Chance fishing were already filling his head and the title of grandpa didn't seem nearly as distasteful as it had in the past.

Walking into the jail, Gideon found Finnie sitting with a man dressed in a suit. The sheriff didn't have to be told that he was about to be introduced to someone from the bank. Gideon could practically smell money.

Rising to his feet, the man offered his hand. "Sheriff, I'm Eldon Hopkins. I've been sent from Denver to manage the bank," he said.

"Welcome to Last Stand, Mr. Hopkins. How can I help you?" Gideon asked.

"I heard this morning that you had returned and I wanted to let you know that after auditing the books, I have determined the bank was robbed of twenty thousand dollars. Obviously, I have a lot of nervous customers that are concerned about their money," Eldon said.

Studying the banker, Gideon tried to decide if he was going to like the man. Mr. Hopkins appeared too formal and stiff for Last Stand. Mr. Fredrick had been the perfect banker for the town and would be sorely missed. Gideon doubted the same sentiment would be felt for the new man.

"We recovered a lot of loot. I'll have to find out how much money they stole from the train before I know if it is all here," Gideon said.

"I see. That's good to know. I think you should know that the board back in Denver is considering shutting down this bank. They have serious concerns over your ability to protect the bank and its customer's wealth," Mr. Hopkins said.

"Well, there's not much I can do about your board. I lost two people that I liked and admired during this robbery. That's my main concern. If you pull up stakes, there'll be somebody else that comes in and starts a new bank. Tell your board that it'll be their loss," Gideon said and walked around Mr. Hopkins to his desk and sat down in his chair.

Mr. Hopkins stood facing the door with his back to the lawmen. He paused for a moment before striding out the door.

"You look considerably better," Gideon said to Finnie.

"You too. I feel like a new man," Finnie said as he rubbed his hand over his smoothly shaved cheeks. "A real bed can do wonders even if Mary's belly takes up most of the room."

"That could get you killed," Gideon warned.

"Not if she doesn't know. By the way, I already sent a telegram to try to get confirmation on the railroad's loss," Finnie said.

"Well, look at you. You'll probably run against me in the next election. I'm apparently not too popular right now anyways," Gideon said.

"Everybody will get over it when they get their money back," Finnie said.

"I suppose. I'm more worried about how I feel about it. Do you think I should have done things differently?" Gideon asked.

"Gideon, how many times did we already go over this on the trail? I think the only thing that would've turned out differently was that we wouldn't have had to chase them halfway across the west," Finnie said.

"And Betsy wouldn't have been raped," Gideon said as he tossed his hat onto the desk.

"True, but you tried your best to keep her alive," Finnie said.

Mayor Hiram Howard walked into the jail and sat down beside Finnie. "Gideon, the town is riled up. People are questioning whether you're fit for the job. Between the rustling and letting the robbers run off with the money, everybody is worked up," Hiram said.

"Well, good morning to you too," Gideon said. "I tried to keep Betsy alive. I failed, but I didn't see much choice. I guess it doesn't matter how much good I've done around here. People lose their money and they're ready to turn on me. I got the money back. That's all anybody gives a damn about anyways."

"That's good to hear. That should help quiet them down. I just wanted to let you know how things were. I realize you got stuck between a rock and a hard spot. You know I'll always take up for you," Hiram said.

"So you weren't down on me?" Gideon asked.

"No, certainly not. I admit that I was considerably worried about my money, but I know that you always try your best," Hiram answered. "I got to get back to the store."

As the door closed behind the mayor, Finnie decided to try to change the subject and said, "Tell me about that grandbaby."

Gideon leaned back in his chair and smiled sadly at Finnie. "You know, Finnie, I probably don't show my appreciation enough, but you really are a good friend," he said. "But to answer your question, that baby was just about the sweetest thing I've ever seen."

"Good. I can't wait to see her," Finnie said.

"I'm going to take a walk of the town. I might be gone awhile," Gideon said as he arose from his chair.

As Gideon walked the street, he studied the reactions of the townsfolk to him. Some of the people seemed their normal self, but others avoided eye contact or barely spoke. On a normal day, he would be ready to get back to the office by the time he had finished talking to everyone on his walk, but not today.

Gideon headed down a side street to the home of the retired Sheriff Fuller. He found the old man sitting on his porch smoking a cigar. The former sheriff had once been a strapping man, but time had withered his muscles away. His eyes were still bright and his mind keen and Gideon had sought his counsel on more than one occasion.

"I bet I know what this is about," Sheriff Fuller said. "Glad to see you made it home all in one piece."

"Seems I'm not a very popular person around town," Gideon said as he sat down beside the sheriff in the swing.

"It comes with the job. I've been there before. Being sheriff isn't a popularity contest. It's doing your best to uphold the law," Sheriff Fuller said.

"But maybe I didn't do my best. I don't give a damn whether most people like me or not, but I hate making mistakes and having people think that I'm incompetent," Gideon said.

"Gideon, I heard all about what happened. You made the choice that you thought was best. Maybe it was wrong, but it certainly wasn't negligence. I think you were stuck in a difficult situation. You're a sheriff – not God. Mistakes will be made. Just keep doing your best and the town will get over it," Sheriff Fuller said.

"I don't know what I'd do if I didn't have you to talk to," Gideon said.

"You'd figure things out for yourself just like you did all those years that you were running all around the country and gone from here," Sheriff Fuller said.

Gideon grinned. "I'm not sure I did so well with that. I got to be getting back," he said as he walked off the porch.

Finnie stood at the wall pinning up a new batch of wanted poster when Gideon walked into the jail. Having grown tired of rifling through the stack of papers every time he wanted to look at an outlaw, he had recently taken to putting them on the wall.

"The telegram came back and the railroad is claiming that they lost five thousand dollars in the holdup," Finnie said as he looked over his shoulder at Gideon.

"That comes to twenty-five thousand dollars and we found a little over twenty-six. Interesting. I guess they robbed somewhere else that we don't know about. We'll give the extra money to the banker's widow. That's the least we can do for Mrs. Fredrick," Gideon said.

"You think it'll be okay?" Finnie asked.

"I do. She needs money a lot worse than Colorado does. I'll pay my respects and give it to her," Gideon said.

"All added up, I believe there's two thousand dollars in reward money for Charlie Reilly and his gang," Finnie announced.

"Really? That's good to hear. Why don't we split it with Zack and Blackie? That'll help Blackie for the money he lost being out of work while he recovered," Gideon said.

"Sounds fine to me. I guess I better take the money down to the bank," Finnie said.

"I'll go get you the key out of my saddlebag. Did Mary tell you who got their cattle stolen?" Gideon asked.

"Randall Jenkins," Finnie answered.

"Thanks. I'll ride out to his ranch and talk to him. I'm sure I'll get the pleasure of dealing with one more discontented constituent," Gideon said as he pulled his hat down farther onto his head.

Chapter 15

With supper eaten, Kurt Tanner excused himself from Ethan's table. He thanked Sarah for the meal and said that he had to be on his way. After Kurt left, Abby began clearing the table of dishes, humming while she worked.

"Sarah, I don't know why you think we have to have Kurt stay over for so many meals," Ethan said.

Spinning around towards the table, Sarah said, "I didn't realize that you cared. I was just trying to help your hired hand."

"I know. I just think we're over doing it," Ethan said in a measured voice.

Sarah glared at her husband. Something about his tone of voice struck her as irritating. She wished he would just come out and say what he was driving at instead of beating around the bush. "Before Joann married Zack, we had him over for most every meal. I didn't know there was a difference between our hired hands," she said with her voice rising.

Benjamin looked at his parents and realized that they were about to have a big fight. They seldom quarreled, preferring to make their points with each other by teasing. He could see that wasn't going to be the case this evening. Rising from his chair, he slunk back to his bedroom.

"Zack was different. He was practically family from the moment he showed up here with Gideon. And besides, Zack had a decent upbringing. We could see that he amounted to something," Ethan said defensively.

"Why did you hire Kurt if you don't like him?" Sarah demanded.

"He is a good ranch hand. It's not like there are that many unemployed ones to pick from," Ethan said, his voice growing loud in agitation.

Staring at Ethan, Sarah tried to understand what his concerns were. Ethan was one of the least judgmental people she had ever known. She had a hard time believing what she was hearing.

"I grant you that he doesn't have the best manners or greatest speaking skills, but you're a preacher. Where is your compassion? Don't you think it's our duty to try to better Kurt," Sarah said angrily.

"Yes, it is. I didn't say I wanted to fire him. I just don't want him over for supper as often. You and Mary act like he is your project to make him into the next fine citizen of Last Stand," Ethan said irritably.

"Is this because Gideon doesn't care for him? Are you just following Gideon's lead?" Sarah questioned.

"Goodness, no. Most of my adult life has been spent without Gideon around here. I think I learned how to make my own decisions without him just fine. I can't believe you would say that," Ethan said testily.

"Well, I can't believe what I'm hearing from you either. What is it then?" Sarah demanded.

In a quiet voice, Ethan said, "I don't like him being around Benjamin that much. I always knew that Zack was a good role model, but with Kurt, I just don't know. He might just be rough around the edges and I'm making too much of this and not practicing what I preach. But Benjamin is my main concern. I can minimize how much he is around Kurt while we're working, but not at the table. In time, I may find that this was all nonsense. I just don't know."

Sarah sat down at the table across from Ethan. "Why didn't you just come out and say that in the first place. I think you're wrong and I'm not going to stop trying to help Kurt, but I can at least understand your concerns and respect them for the good of our son," she said.

"I don't know. I guess I took the long way to get there," he said.

"God didn't bring Eve to Adam for companionship. He did it so that Adam could have a brain," Sarah said with a smile as she patted Ethan's hand.

∞

Kurt Tanner rode back to his cabin after having supper with the Oakes family. He quickly changed into some clean clothes and then poured himself a glass of whiskey. Sitting down at the table, he nursed the drink to pass the time. His belly was full and he felt content. Sarah could cook better than anyone he had ever known and her meals were a treat. Thoughts about the meal made him reflect on Ethan. His boss hadn't seemed himself during the meal and he wondered if Ethan might be unhappy with his work. Losing his job was the last thing he needed right now.

At sunset, Kurt decided that it was late enough to go to town and visit the Last Chance. He found the saloon packed with the usual Friday night crowd. Kurt sat down at a table with a couple of cowboys that never bothered to work fulltime for any of the ranchers, but instead took jobs when any of the ranches needed extra hands. Most of the other ranch hands considered them lazy and avoided their company, but Kurt didn't mind.

Delta brought him a beer and he sipped the brew while catching up on all the local news with the two men.

After finishing his beer, Kurt decided to go flirt with Mary at the bar. Even if she was pregnant, she still looked better than just about any other woman in Last Stand did and he liked her sassiness. He couldn't fathom how such a catch had ended up with that little mouthy Irishman. The world just wasn't fair in his view. A man had to look out for himself above all else and that's what he planned to do with his life.

"Aren't you looking pretty tonight," Kurt said and gave Mary his best grin.

"Pretty fat," Mary replied with a smile.

"You wear it well. How do they say it? It becomes you, I believe is how it goes," he said.

"Well, I'll be glad when it becomes a baby and not my belly," she said.

Kurt chuckled at her play on words. "I'm sure. I'll have another beer," he said.

Mary filled the mug and placed it in front of the ranch hand. "You know, Kurt, you should be careful with the company that you keep. I'm not too sure about those two," she said.

"Aw, Danny and Lacey are alright. I grant you that both of them are on the lazy side, but they're both honest enough. Don't you worry, ma'am. I plan to make something of myself. I don't hang around shady characters," he said.

"That's good to know. A person can go far if they set their mind to it and I think you're one of those people. I sure never thought I'd own two businesses," Mary said.

Kurt and Mary continued talking until he finished his beer. He ordered another one and then excused himself to make the rounds. The time had come to talk up the other cowboys and play some cards. Kurt loved to listen to the others gossip and complain about the ranch where they worked and to take their money at the card table. Both money and information were things that he found very useful.

Chapter 16

A week had passed since Gideon and Finnie's return from killing the outlaws. News of the return of the bank money had gone a long ways in appeasing the mood of the town though Gideon still got the sense that the shine of his badge had diminished in the eyes of many people. Nonetheless, he and the deputy remained grateful for a quiet week in which to recover from their long journey.

Gideon made his morning walk of the town. The summer sun was already knocking the chill out of the air and the sky looked cloudless and robin egg blue. That morning he had gotten out of bed feeling like his old self again for the first time since returning and he walked with a spring in his step down the street. Just as he returned to the jail, Marcus Hanson rode up.

Seeing Marcus instantly put a damper on Gideon's spirit. There could be no way that the rancher stopped at the jail for a friendly visit. Marcus had once been married to Abby and was Winnie's father. He and Gideon were the same age and had gone to school together. Even back then, they had never been particularly close. Gideon respected Marcus's honesty and work ethic, but considered his personality to be about two shades more engaging than a fence post. After Abby divorced Marcus and married Gideon, the animosity between the two men had grown considerably. And now that Winnie no longer resented Gideon, but considered him a second father, Marcus had become downright hostile towards Gideon and Abby.

"I need to talk to you," Marcus said as he climbed down from his horse.

Gideon's first inclination was to wonder what Winnie had said to her father on her last visit to see him. Winnie could be a willful child and there was no telling what she might have said if she had been upset with Abby.

"Come on in," Gideon said, walking into the jail and sitting down at his desk.

Marcus followed and dropped into a chair in front of the sheriff. He sat hunched over with his legs wide apart and his arms dangling against his thighs. "I've been having a ranch hand stay with each of my herds since you can't seem to find the rustlers and had to go chase bank robbers across the country that you let get away. Reese never came in this morning and I went looking for him. I found him dead and my cattle gone," he said.

Sitting back in his chair, Gideon rubbed his scar and inhaled deeply before blowing out the air with his cheeks puffed up. The news surprised him too much to bother being irritated at Marcus's insults. "I liked Reese and I'm sorry to hear that. When's the last time that you saw him?" he asked.

"Three day ago," Marcus answered.

"Three days ago? I know your spread is big, but it's not so big that you couldn't have had your men come check in each day. What kind of fool does something like that? That's the silliest damn thing I've ever heard tell," Gideon challenged.

"I'll tell you what kind of fool does that – one that thinks he has an incompetent sheriff," Marcus said as he arose to his feet.

"Well, I'd say you're the one that looks pretty incompetent at this moment," Gideon said as he stood up and leaned over the desk, bracing his arms to support his weight.

"You love this, don't you? I'm sure you can't wait to get home to bad mouth me to Winnie," Marcus hollered.

"I've never once said a disparaging word about you to Winnie and I never will. I don't need to do that to win her affection," Gideon said.

Finnie had walked into the jail and sized up the situation. "Gentlemen, I suggest that you take your seats. Neither of your reputations will be well served if you two get into a brawl. Winnie will be the one that suffers," he said.

Gideon glared over at his deputy before sitting down and Marcus followed his lead.

"We've got a murder on our hands and some cattle rustled from Marcus's place," Gideon said to Finnie.

"Then I suggest we get out there and have a look," Finnie said.

"It could have happened three days ago," Gideon said with disdain in his voice while looking at Marcus.

"Will we need a wagon to bring the body back?" Finnie asked.

"No, I'll bury Reese on the ranch. He doesn't have any family around these here parts and apparently had a checkered past. We never could pin him down on where he came from," Marcus said as he stood again.

The three men took the road south to Marcus's ranch and then headed east to the body. A trail of blood stretched for fifty yards from the remains and forced Gideon to look away for a moment to steel himself for the job at hand. He climbed down from the horse and flipped over the body. Reese had a gunshot to the chest that had apparently severed a major artery. Animals had nearly gnawed an arm off and chewed a gaping hole in his thigh. After being shot, the ranch hand had walked and crawled back towards the ranch before succumbing to his injuries. His horse also lay dead.

"I haven't seen this much blood since the war," Finnie remarked.

"Poor Reese. He really was a pretty fair ranch hand. He'd calmed down a lot in the last few years. He sure never deserved to go like this," Marcus said before setting his jaw in a grimace.

"I would say he's been dead for two, if not three days. Let's try to figure out how many of them there were," Gideon said and started walking around the pasture.

The men walked around for a few minutes scanning the ground.

"I come up with three horses. What about you?" Finnie asked.

"Same thing. I'd say we're probably dealing with the same ones that stole Carter Mason's cattle and Randall Jenkins' herd while we were gone. They drove the herd east just like before," Gideon said and spat on the ground.

"Except that this time they got bold enough to murder," Finnie said.

"Yes, they did and I'd swear they have inside information on each of their thefts. Each one took days before anybody realized they'd been robbed," Gideon said.

"I thought the same thing," Finnie said.

"Marcus, we're done here. Are you going to take care of Reese's body?" Gideon asked.

"Yeah, I'll get him buried. Gideon, I want to apologize for what I said earlier. I was upset with Reese's murder and I took it out on you. I'm truly sorry," Marcus said.

"We're good. And Marcus, I'd never try to turn Winnie against you," Gideon said.

"I know," Marcus replied.

"Have you gone to see Joann's baby? She's a cute little thing," Gideon said.

"No, I haven't been out there in a while," Marcus answered.

"Abby told me after I got back that Joann mentioned that you hadn't been out yet. She thinks the world of you. You need to go. You're part of her family too," Gideon said.

Marcus smiled and held his hand out to shake with Gideon.

"I'll get out there and see the baby. The past is in the past. I'm going to let go of it. No more hard feelings," Marcus said as they shook hands.

"I'd like that," Gideon said.

Gideon and Finnie departed and began the journey back to town.

"This has been a strange day," Finnie said as they rode.

"Tell me about it. I was in a good mood. If you hadn't walked into the jail when you did, I fear Marcus and I would have come to blows. And we have to get this rustling stopped before somebody else dies. Nobody is going to keep this stealing up right under our noses," Gideon said.

Once back in town, Finnie said, "I'm going to make a walk of the town. It can't hurt for everybody to see we're still on the job."

"That'll be good. I'm going to talk to your wife. She's the best detective in this town," Gideon said.

Walking into the Last Chance, Gideon sat down at his usual table and waited for Mary to bring him a beer. She busied herself slicing meat as Delta brought out food for the lunch crowd and didn't notice him for a moment. When she did, she grabbed a mug and filled it.

"Are you ever going to have that baby?" Gideon asked as she walked over to him.

"Doc says it could be anytime now. I'm ready," Mary said.

"Can you sit down for a minute?" he asked.

Mary looked back towards the bar, before answering. "Your timing isn't the greatest, but Delta can finish up," she said.

Gideon jumped up and pulled a chair out for her, helping her scoot up to the table.

"Marcus had some cattle rustled and Reese was murdered," Gideon said.

"Oh, no, that's terrible. I liked Reese. He always behaved himself in here. Somebody is sure getting brazen," Mary said.

"Exactly. It's as if they know that the cattle herd won't be checked on for a few days. Have you seen anything suspicious with your customers?" he asked.

"Gideon, I have a whole room full of cowboys in here on Friday and Saturday nights. Some of them are good and some of them aren't, but they all mingle with each other. There hasn't been anybody new in town or anything that stands out in my mind," she said.

"That's not what I wanted to hear. I thought with your ability to see the good and evil in men that you'd have some ideas for me. You're the best lawman in town," Gideon said before taking a drink of beer.

"Well, Deputy Mary is at a loss this time. I don't know what to tell you," she said before putting her hand to her stomach and wincing.

"Are you okay?" Gideon asked with concern.

"Yeah, the baby just gave me a real good kick. Want to feel?" Mary said.

Gideon rested his hand on Mary's stomach and smiled. "I never grew tired of feeling Chance kick Abby. There's something about it that is so miraculous," he said.

"Spoken like a true man. You wouldn't think it was so great if it happened to you constantly," she said.

"Oh, just be glad that baby is showing you that it's alive and healthy," Gideon said.

"I am. I'm just teasing. Don't be so literal. I couldn't stand you getting all serious on me now," Mary said.

"Well, I'm going to be serious one more time. I want you to know how happy I am for you and Finnie. I can't think of two people that deserve happiness more than you two," he said.

Mary smiled and patted Gideon's hand. "Thank you. Me, you, and Finnie have had more changes in our lives in the last few years than the rest of the town put together," she said.

"Have you picked out names yet? Finnie won't answer me," Gideon said.

"We have a boy's name picked out, but I can't tell you. We agreed to keep it a secret. We're still fighting over what to call a girl," Mary said.

"That sounds about right. That knot-head husband of yours would probably name a girl something awful if you let him," he said.

"You can only imagine what he's come up with. Some of them sound like Irish witch names to me," Mary said and giggled.

Chapter 17

Gideon had kept postponing the conversation he needed to have with Abby the previous night until he missed his opportunity when she fell asleep. As they sat eating breakfast the next morning, he waited for the right moment to speak. He knew that she wouldn't be happy and he dreaded ruining the morning.

"Abby, I've decided to go stay in Alamosa at the hotel for a few days to keep an eye on the railyard. It's the only way that I can think of to maybe catch the rustlers. I know the cattle are getting shipped out there," Gideon said.

Abby set her fork down and looked at her husband. "Gideon, you've been gone more than you've been here lately. The children need you. I need you. Can't you come up with something else?" she asked.

"I wish I could. I don't fancy the idea of being away from home either. My own bed suits me just fine, but I got to put a stop to this rustling before somebody else gets killed. These rustlers are good at what they do," he said.

"Is it going to be like this forever?" Abby asked.

"Abby, you know that sometimes months go by with nothing more than a drunk getting rowdy. Now is not one of those times," Gideon said.

"How are you going to know whether a herd is rustled or not?" Abby asked.

"I've been back in Last Stand long enough that I think I know all the brands and the cowboys that go with them. And if I don't, I'll use my keen sense of observation to spot the bad guys," Gideon said, smiling at his attempt at humor.

Peering at Gideon, Abby said, "You're lucky that you're so charming or I might start looking to replace you. And on a similar subject, you never gave me any details with how you and Marcus got along."

Glancing across the room to make sure that Winnie remained preoccupied with playing with Chance, Gideon said, "It started out badly. We nearly came to blows, but things ended on good terms. In fact, I think we came to an understanding where things will be a lot better from here on out."

"Good. We have several more years of dealing with Marcus until Winnie gets grown and it's time for everybody to move on. Let's go pack you some clothes," she said before she shoved her last bite of bacon into her mouth.

After packing and telling the family goodbye, Gideon rode to town. Finnie already knew of his plans and after Gideon spent a few minutes with the deputy, he walked across the street to see the doctor. Doc had been so busy with his family that Gideon had barely seen him lately. He found the doctor sitting at his desk doing paperwork.

"So the town does still have a doctor," Gideon said.

"Yes, people are complaining about me about as much as they are about the sheriff. Our popularity is on the wane," Doc said.

"They'll like us again the first time that they need us," Gideon said as he sat down in a chair.

"Oh, I know. The family leaves in a week and I'm already dreading it. I've grown more attached to those grandkids than I ever thought possible. I still can't fathom how it all happened, but they're just so darn enjoyable to be around," Doc said and rubbed his chin.

"Well, I can. I would be content to sit and hold Tess all day. You're just not the crusty old heartless doctor that you like everybody to think you are," Gideon said.

Doc smiled and pulled off his glasses. "I suppose, but I never claimed to be heartless, just crusty," he said and chuckled.

"I'm going to be gone a few days. I'll probably miss out on Mary having her baby like I did Joann," Gideon said.

"Good God, you'd think you were married to her. I'm surprised Finnie puts up with you. She'll be fine," Doc said.

"Don't say that in front of Abby," Gideon said.

"Abby already knows. She loves you anyway and somehow understands your friendship with Mary. Not many women would under similar circumstances," Doc said.

"Crusty. Crusty. Crusty. I got to go," Gideon said as he arose from his seat.

"Be careful," Doc warned.

Not being in a particular hurry, Gideon rode the thirty some miles to Alamosa at an easy pace. Buck had put some of his weight back on and had to be reined in to keep from racing most of the way there. Gideon slipped his badge into his pocket before reaching the town in the afternoon. He rode straight to the hotel and checked in under an alias. Once finished there, Gideon walked down the street to the sheriff's office.

The sheriff sat in front of the jail reading a newspaper when Gideon walked up to him.

"Sheriff Johann, what can I do for you?" the sheriff asked.

"Can we talk inside your office?" Gideon asked.

"Sure," Sheriff White said before folding his newspaper and walking into the jail.

"I'm going to be hanging around the railyard for a few days to see if any rustled cattle from Last Stand come in. I'm still having problems with rustlers and I know they're bringing the herds here to be shipped. I'm staying at the hotel and I'm not letting anybody know I'm a sheriff," Gideon said.

"Suit yourself and good luck. I hope you have better luck than I'm having. I'm still dealing with rustlers myself. Maybe they're the same ones," the sheriff said.

"Could be. I'm going to get out of here before somebody sees me with you. I'll come get you if I find something," Gideon said.

"Thanks for the heads-up. You be careful," Sheriff White said.

Alamosa was only a slightly bigger town than Last Stand and staying inconspicuous would be the challenge. Gideon walked down to the railyard and covertly looked around, finding only empty cattle pens. With nothing else to do, he walked back to Buck and rode a wide circle around the town until his belly began growling too loudly to ignore. He dropped the horse off at the livery stable before dining alone at the hotel. Fearing he might be recognized at a saloon, Gideon retired to his room. Twice during the evening, he walked down to the pens. Though too dark to see, the quiet convinced him that no cattle occupied the pens. He gladly went to bed to end his boredom.

Gideon awoke in the morning at the first sign of light. He waited for the restaurant to open and downed a breakfast of ham, eggs, and biscuits. Afterwards, he made another trip to the railyard. No cattle were in sight. Spending the day loitering proved to be about as exciting as watching grass grow as well as a challenge not to appear obvious in his mission. A herd came in from the north after lunch. The direction of their arrival was wrong and the cattle looked to be old stock that hadn't calved in the spring. Waiting until after five o'clock, Gideon traipsed back to the hotel for dinner.

While looking over the menu, Gideon could feel eyes watching him. Before looking up, he reached under the table to make sure he could draw his gun if necessary. He glanced up and saw the railroad detective and the livestock clerk standing near the doorway staring at him. When he made eye contact with them, they marched to his table.

"I thought I saw you hanging around today. What do you think you're doing?" the detective demanded.

"I didn't know it was a crime to be in Alamosa," Gideon said.

"You better not set foot in the railyard. That's private property and your badge don't carry no weight around here. I'll take a club to you if you do," the detective warned.

"And I'll blow a hole in that pinhead of yours if you try it," Gideon threatened.

"I'm going to let the sheriff know that you're here. I don't imagine he'd take kindly to you prying about in his town," the detective warned.

"You'd be wasting your time. He already knows I'm here. I'm about to have me some dinner. If you two don't get away from my table, I'm going to waylay both of you," Gideon said and stared at the detective.

The clerk took a step backwards, but the detective held his ground and continued the stare down. Gideon stood quickly, sending his chair shooting back into the customer at the next table. With his hand resting on his Colt, he waited for the detective's next move.

"You damn Yankees think you rule the world. This isn't over with by a long shot," the detective said before awkwardly spinning around and limping out the door with the clerk close on his heels.

Gideon wanted to punch something. He had hoped that the detective would go for his gun or nightstick. Nothing would have given him more pleasure than to lay his gun upside the old Confederate's head. He apologized to the man behind him as the waitress walked over to the table. He ordered a steak. When the meal came, he gobbled the food down without bothering to notice the taste in his agitated state. After paying for his meal, he checked out of the hotel and walked to the livery stable. Staying in Alamosa any longer would be futile. He would ride home that night stewing on the fact that the crooked railroad detective had bested him.

Chapter 18

Surprised at seeing Buck tied outside the jail, Finnie walked in to find Gideon asleep on the cot. The sheriff stirred at the sound of the bell above the door and sat up on the bed.

"Top of the morning to you. I didn't expect to see you here," Finnie said as he walked to the stove to start making coffee.

"That damn railroad detective spotted me. That's a hard place to be inconspicuous in," Gideon said.

"You must have stood out like a whorehouse between two churches with the barely clad girls waving at the men from the balcony on Sunday morning," Finnie said as he struck a match.

"Something like that. I knew there'd be no rustling with the detective and that clerk knowing that I was hanging around so I just rode back last night. By the time I got here I felt tired and I feared that if I showed up at my door that Abby might shoot first and ask questions later," Gideon said.

"Yeah, it would make a bad ending to the exploits of the legendary Gideon Johann if he was accidentally killed by his wife," Finnie teased.

"The ending is going to be bad enough if we don't catch these rustlers," Gideon remarked.

"So what now?" Finnie asked.

"They have to know that they have a couple of days to get rid of the cattle. I still think they're getting their information at the saloon. Try to see what goes on when you're in there. Mary will be doing the same," Gideon answered.

"I'm good at hanging out in saloons," Finnie said.

"After I have a cup of your coffee, I'm going home for the day. I think I'll have Doc bring his family out this afternoon so that John and Henry can shoot a gun before they leave. I'm sure Abby will appreciate me inviting company over on such short notice," Gideon said with a grin as he walked over to the gun cabinet to retrieve some cartridges.

Once finished with his coffee, Gideon headed home to find Abby so happy at his early return that she welcomed the idea of company. He killed a couple of their chickens and helped Abby scald and pluck the birds. By the time that Doc and his family arrived, Abby and Winnie had all the food prepared for cooking.

John Hamilton proved useless with a gun. After the Winchester rifle kicked him on his first shot, he would flinch his shoulder back each time as he squeezed the trigger and his shot would miss the mark by a wide margin. Henry had natural ability with a rifle and once he got the hang of shooting, he could put his shot within six inches of the bull's eye and hit dead center twice. Neither the father nor son had much success with the Colt revolver. Gideon explained that shooting a pistol took years of practice. He finished off the shooting by drawing his revolver from its holster and rapidly hitting five of the six cans sitting on the corral fence. Duly impressed with Gideon's shooting, Doc led the procession back to the cabin for supper.

John kept rubbing his shoulder during the meal and complaining about the bruise he knew he had, but Henry wouldn't stop talking excitedly about the guns.

"Maybe I should become a policeman in Boston," Henry said.

"Whoa, there," Gideon said. "A smart boy like you needs to go to school to become a banker or a doctor. Those bullets hurt when they hit you. Ask your dad. You can shoot guns as a hobby."

"Are you going to miss Last Stand?" Abby asked Kate.

"You know, I am. I miss many things about Boston, but there is a lot to love here too. It's a wild and wooly place, but I can see how it gets in your blood. I now know why John insisted that the family come here for a visit. And then there's Doc. Meeting him has been so good for the children and me too. I'd say I have the perfect father-in-law," Kate gushed.

"You need to leave soon then, because Doc is kind of like drinking fine whiskey. It's good until you have too much and then it makes you sick," Gideon said as he smirked at the doctor.

Doc shook his head and looked at Abby as if she should have better control of her husband.

∞

Zack came home late from working for Ethan. They had spent the day culling and separating the herds. Ethan was particular when it came to selecting heifers to keep back for breeding and Zack had worked with the rancher long enough to know what he looked for in an animal. Occasionally they had a lively debate over a heifer, but Zack could see that Ethan was proud of the eye his hired hand had developed for cattle.

Joann met him at the door and handed him Tess.

"Hold her while I start supper. She's fussy today. How was your day?" Joann said.

"It was long, but good, and I'm tired. We got the cattle sorted to Ethan's satisfaction," Zack answered.

"What do you think of Kurt?" Joann asked as she walked to the stove.

"I don't know. Sarah sure has taken a shine to him. I think she sees him as her project to polish. Most times he seems like a decent enough fellow that didn't have much upbringing and then every once in a while he'll say something that makes me think that he's way more calculating than he lets on," he said.

"I think Daddy has misgivings about him too. He and Sarah usually agree on everything. Probably even more than he and Abs do," Joann said.

"That's because he's not married to Sarah. Everybody has to disagree with their spouse to keep things interesting," Zack said.

"So is that why you're so disagreeable – to keep things interesting?" she teased.

"If that's not the pot calling the kettle black I don't know what is," he said.

"Be careful or I'll be serving you shoe leather for supper," Joann warned.

"Tess feels warm to me and her nose is running," Zack said.

Joann walked over and laid her hand on the baby's forehead. "Maybe a little. She's probably getting a summer cold. I'll keep an eye on her," she said.

Chapter 19

Rising at first light, Zack followed his new routine of taking a lamp over to Tess to check on his daughter. Looking down into the bassinet, Tess's face appeared flushed bright red. Zack reached down and put his palm to her forehead. Her skin felt as if she had been left out under the sun on a hot day. He didn't know much about babies, but he knew his daughter had a high fever.

"Joann, get over here. Tess is burning up," Zack called out, concern coloring his voice.

The new mother awoke with a start, climbing out of bed she rushed over, tripping on Zack's boots and nearly falling before reaching her daughter. She picked up the baby and held the infant's face against her cheek.

"Get me a bowl of water and a rag. I'm going to try to cool her down," she said as she began removing the baby's nightgown.

The cold water woke up the baby, but even with the shock of the wet rag, she didn't cry and acted lethargic.

"I better go get Doc," Zack said.

"Yes, I think we need him," Joann said as she offered Tess a breast that the baby refused to suckle.

Zack saddled his horse and made the journey to town as quickly as possible. The doctor's office sat empty and he walked across the street to the jail where he found Doc sitting with Gideon sipping coffee. The two men sat slumped in their seats obviously relaxed in the presence of each other's company.

"Tess has a fever and won't eat. I think you need to come check her," Zack blurted out.

"Okay, calm down. I'm sure she'll be fine," Doc said as he stood.

"When did it start?" Gideon asked.

"Joann said that she was fussy yesterday and she felt a little warm last night, but this morning she felt downright hot. She doesn't look good," Zack said.

"I'll get my buggy and be right out," Doc said as he departed.

Zack stood looking at Gideon. The young man's posture wasn't its normal ramrod straight bearing and he had his hands shoved into his pockets. He had the appearance of carrying all the weight of the world on his shoulders.

Gideon felt the need to reassure his son-in-law. "Abby and I will ride over this evening and check on things. I doubt it's as bad as it seems," he said.

"I'm going to go on and head back. I know Joann is scared," Zack said.

"Try not to worry and I'll see you later," Gideon said.

Returning home ahead of the doctor, Zack found Joann still wiping the baby down to try to reduce her temperature. His wife's forehead was furrowed with concern and her mouth drawn tightly shut in a grimace that he had never seen from her before now.

"Is she any better?" Zack asked.

"No, she won't nurse and she has a cough. I'm worried, Zack," Joann said.

"Both Doc and Gideon said that we're probably getting worked up over nothing," he said.

"I don't know. She's pretty sick and babies are so helpless. I can't bear to think of something happening to her," Joann said.

Zack sat down beside Joann and put his arm around her shoulders. He felt at a loss for words to reassure his wife and could only say, "Doc, will be here soon."

The doctor arrived a short time later and ambled up to the door. He let himself in and walked over to the couple. "Is her fever still up?" he asked as he set his bag down and rummaged through its contents until he found his stethoscope.

"I fear so. I keep wiping her down with a wet rag," Joann answered.

Doc patiently moved his stethoscope over Tess's chest as he listened to her heart and lungs. Retrieving his thermometer, the five minutes that elapsed to record her temperature seemed like forever.

"Her heart sounds good, but her lungs are congested. She has a temperature of one hundred and three," Doc announced. "You have a sick little girl on your hands."

"Is she going to be alright?" Zack asked.

"I think so. I have some medicine that we'll give her," Doc said.

"I can't get her to eat," Joann said and started to sniffle.

Doc rested his hand on Joann's shoulder. "You're getting yourself all worked up before you have a reason to be. All babies get sick," he said.

The doctor pulled out bottles from his bag of a tincture made from willow bark and another of onion syrup. He asked for a spoon and then deftly administered a teaspoon of each into Tess's mouth. The baby puckered up, but swallowed the medicines.

"Fix me some coffee. Zack interrupted my cup this morning. I'll stick around for a while and see if the fever goes down. You'll need to give Tess a teaspoon from each bottle once every four hours," Doc said.

Zack went to make the coffee while Joann cradled the baby.

"When is your family headed back east?" Joann asked.

"In three days. I'm dreading it. I've gotten used to having them around all the time. Those grandkids are something else. I sure never thought they'd wrap me around their little fingers like they have. Rose is just so full of life that she draws you into her world and Tad is so darn cute that I can't help but to want to spoil him. Henry is smart. That boy is going places. John and Kate have done a fine job of raising them. I've grown quite fond of Kate also. She keeps John on his toes," Doc gushed.

"They're a fine family and I can see why you're so proud. I wish I could have spent more time with them, but I'll never forget the four kids traipsing up to the cabin all soaking wet. They played that one well," she said and smiled as the memory allowed her to forget her worries for a moment.

"They certainly did," Doc said with a chuckle as the baby coughed.

"Doc, are you sure Tess is going to be okay?" Joann asked.

"You can never be for sure in medicine, but I feel confident that she will be. I wouldn't leave if I felt otherwise," he said.

Zack returned with the coffee and they all sat around the table drinking a cup. Doc passed the time telling stories on Gideon, Abby, and Ethan in their youth. He had the worried couple giggling by the time that the cups were empty.

After an hour had passed, Doc took the baby's temperature again. Her fever had dropped to one hundred and one.

"I'm going to return to town. I'll be back in the morning and if you need me before then, come and get me. That's why I'm here," Doc said as he stuffed his instruments back into the bag.

After the doctor departed, the couple sat across from each other at the table unable to think of anything to say.

Finally, Joann said, "Go on and get some work done. I'll be fine by myself. Doc made me feel better about Tess. Maybe I'll get her to eat when she wakes."

"I forgot to tell you that Gideon said that they'd come over this evening to check on us," Zack said.

"Good. Fevers tend to rise at night," she said.

Zack left to work on clearing some acreage while Joann kept watch over the baby. Tess slept most of the day and Joann had to wake her to give her the medicine. Just before starting dinner, Joann coxed Tess to nurse briefly. By the time Zack returned home, supper was nearly cooked and the baby slept.

"How is she doing?" Zack asked as he hung his hat on its peg.

"I don't think her fever has gone back up and I got her to nurse a little. My breasts feel like they're going to erupt," Joann said as she put her hand to her chest.

"We wouldn't want that," Zack said with a smile.

"You might as well get your mind off that for all the good in this world it will do you. You haven't even mentioned how much weight I've lost," she said.

"Don't think I haven't noticed. I was just waiting to mention it when it would do me some good in this world," he said and grinned.

"Men. Thank goodness Sarah told me what you were all like," Joann said as she turned back to the stove.

Relieved to see the tension gone from his wife's face, Zack checked on Tess before sitting down at the table to wait for supper. Zack rattled on about how much land he cleared that day as they ate and by the time they had finished the meal, Gideon, Abby, and the kids had arrived.

"How is that grandbaby of mine?" Abby asked as she barged towards the baby's bassinet.

"She's better than she was, but I've still barely got her to eat," Joann answered.

Abby picked up Tess and cuddled the child's head against her cheek. "She feels pretty warm to me," she said.

Joann walked over and laid the back of her hand against the baby's cheek. "Her temperature is rising again. She's due for medicine in ten minutes. I'll go ahead and give her some," she said.

After administering the medicine, Joann took the baby to the bedroom to nurse. She returned ten minutes later. "She won't eat," she said dejectedly.

An hour passed and the medicine failed to bring Tess's fever down and her breathing made a rattling sound. Abby felt the baby's forehead and thought her temperature may have even risen higher.

"I'll wipe her down with a wet rag again," Joann said as she poured water from a pitcher into a bowl.

"I think somebody needs to go get Doc. Tess is too young to carry that much fever for a long time and the medicine doesn't seem to be working," Abby announced.

Gideon stood. "I'll go. Zack can stay here with his baby and I'll take his horse," he said.

Traveling as fast as he dared with dusk settling in, Gideon found Doc in the Last Chance purveying gossip. The doctor tipped back his beer and drained it before walking to his office to get his bag while the sheriff went to the stable to get the buggy hitched. Gideon tied his horse behind the carriage and rode back to the cabin with the doctor.

As soon as Gideon entered the cabin, he could see that things were not good. Joann sat rocking Tess as the infant cried at the top of her lungs. Abby paced the floor. Chance slept in front of the fireplace. Zack and Winnie sat at the table looking lost.

The doctor again listened to the baby's chest and then took her temperature. "Her fever has hit one hundred and four and her lungs don't sound any better. I'm going to give her a different medicine. I don't like giving it to babies, but we don't have much choice," he said as he fished a bottle out of his bag.

"Doc, you have to help her," Joann cried out.

"I'm trying, Joann," he said as he dumped a teaspoon of medicine into Tess's mouth. "Wipe her down with the rag again."

The cold rag made the baby scream until she cried herself to sleep. Much to Joann's displeasure, the doctor insisted that Tess be laid down in her bed so that she didn't absorb her mother's body heat. Doc sat down at the table and watched the clock as it seemed to take forever to reach the forty-five minutes so that he could take her temperature again.

Tess had not responded to the medicine and her fever remained unchanged. The doctor looked around the room at the faces peering back at him. He wasn't sure what to say. For the first time, he worried that Tess's condition appeared grave.

"She's unchanged. I don't have anything else to offer. We'll keep cooling her with a rag. It might be time to start praying," Doc said and began rubbing his chin trying to think of something more encouraging to say.

Joann and Abby hugged each other and started crying. Winnie followed suit at seeing her sister and mother in tears. Zack sat too stunned to express any emotion while Gideon paced the room.

Needing to get away, Gideon walked outside and sat down on the swing. Doc followed and sat down beside him.

"She's not going to make it, is she?" Gideon asked.

"She's not a lost cause, but that fever needs to break. It worries me that the medicine isn't helping and that she's not eating. She'll dehydrate," Doc said.

"Life's not fair, is it?" Gideon said.

"No, never has been and never will be. We have to play the hand we're dealt and some never even get the chance to play. It's best to guard your aces," Doc said.

A sigh escaped Gideon. "I'm going for a walk," he said.

"In the dark?" Doc asked.

"I've spent a good portion of my life there," Gideon said before trotting off the porch.

Gideon wasn't sure he could keep his emotions in check and wanted to be alone in case he failed. He walked down to the stream and listened to the water breaking over the rocks. The sound made him think of the years that he'd wasted running aimlessly. Returning to Last Stand had saved him and he'd come to believe that God had his hand in his life's changes. He wondered why God would now bring such a precious little baby into the world only to snatch Tess away a couple of weeks later. The magnitude of his love for Tess amazed Gideon. It wasn't that he loved her more than he loved his own kids, but there was something so liberating in loving a grandchild. Desperate to save the baby, he got down on his knees in prayer to offer his life in return for the survival of Tess. The tears ran down his cheeks and he felt as if they had washed away his burden. Walking back to the cabin, he had faith.

The cabin seemed so quiet when Gideon entered that he could almost believe the home sat empty. Tess, Chance, and Winnie slept. Everyone else sat scattered about the room looking lost. Gideon made a point of squatting beside each of his family and encouraged them to keep faith that Tess would be fine. Abby and Joann seemed too lost in worry to really hear his words. Zack listened and nodded his head.

Throughout the night, Doc gave the baby medicine and Abby and Joann took turns wiping Tess down with the wet cloth. Abby finally convinced Zack and Joann to go take a nap and Gideon fell asleep sitting in a chair.

Sitting down beside Doc, Abby said, "It's in God's hands now, isn't it?"

"It is," Doc answered as he pulled off his spectacles.

"That poor little baby. And poor Zack and Joann too. I don't know if Joann is strong enough to handle this," she said.

"She's got your and Gideon's fire in her. She'll be alright," Doc said.

"I don't know. We didn't raise her. Uncle Jake and Aunt Rita are such gentle souls. I don't know if she's got our grit," Abby mused.

"Let's just hope that things are better in the light of morning," Doc said.

The sun had barely peeked above the horizon when everybody began to stir. The family crowded around the doctor as he examined Tess. He put his stethoscope to her chest and listened. Her heartbeat had grown faint and her lungs sounded terrible. He didn't need to take her temperature. Forty plus years of doctoring had taught him that the baby was fading. Babies never bounced back when they had deteriorated to the point where Tess had now arrived. Breaking the news was all that remained to be done.

Doc pulled off his spectacles and rubbed his chin. He looked up at the expectant eyes staring at him and shook his head. "I'm sorry, but Tess is fading. There's nothing left to do," he said.

Joann let out a wail that awakened Winnie and Chance. The children huddled on the floor with Winnie wrapping her arms around her little brother in a protective bear hug. Zack took his wife into his arms and tried to hug the pain away.

Pushing away from Zack, Joann said, "Ethan. Somebody has to get Ethan. I want Tess baptized."

Using his sleeve to wipe his eyes, Gideon said, "I'll go. I probably should have let them know what was going on before now." He made a quick exit out the door.

Gideon returned with Ethan and his family a short time later. After the Oakes family consoled everyone, Joann picked up Tess while Ethan began the baptism. The baby's breathing had grown shallow and she no longer opened her eyes. Ethan sprinkled the holy water onto Tess and then led a prayer.

Joann sat down in the rocker that Zack had surprised her with after Tess had been born. She rocked the child and sang lullabies. Zack sat on the fireplace hearth beside his wife, looking childlike and lost. Everyone else stood around not knowing what to say. The situation felt too dire to talk of anything else and nobody wanted to talk about what was happening before their eyes.

The rocking went on for nearly an hour until Tess had taken her last breath. Joann called out to Doc. The doctor walked over with his stethoscope and listen one more time to Tess's chest.

"She's gone," he said with his voice breaking.

With a wail so shrill that the noise felt ear piercing, Joann swaddled Tess against her chest and rocked her daughter. Scared from the tortured sounds, Winnie, Chance, and even Benjamin began crying, causing Sarah to lead the children outside to talk to them. Zack sat motionless and seemed too in shock to mourn. Gideon's world was crumbling and Abby wrapped her arms around him before he could bolt for the door. She found herself in the rare spot of having to be the strong one and tried to comfort him. Through his tears, Gideon mumbled indecipherable words into her shoulder.

"I have to go outside," Gideon said pushed away from Abby.

He walked outside past Sarah and the children sitting on the steps and headed for the stream. The sunlight was so bright that he had to squint and he wondered how the world could look so sunny without Tess in it. Standing where the water made a pool, he watched the water break over the natural dam. As he stood there, he could hear footsteps approaching and knew the sounds came from Ethan without having to look.

"Why?" Gideon asked without turning his head as Ethan came up beside him.

"I don't know," Ethan answered.

"Ethan, I had so much faith last night that Tess would be better today. What does the faith of a mustard seed moving mountains mean then? Why bring a child into the world for a couple of weeks only to snatch her away?" Gideon asked.

"I think that sometimes God has other plans from what we think we need. Why that would involve taking Tess, I don't know. It's hard to find a good answer with a child's death. Maybe Heaven needed Tess more than we did," Ethan said.

"Maybe God had a plan for me to get my life turned around so that he could bring pain to my whole family for me killing that boy and the sorrow I brought upon his family," Gideon said.

"No. No. No. You paid for that accident a hundred times over and you saved Benjamin's life. I refuse to believe that our God is a spiteful God," Ethan said.

"I just don't know anymore," Gideon said.

"You've come too far to ever go back to the way things were. Time will heal this terrible burden. You have to have faith that this is all part of God's plan no matter how wrong it seems. There's really no other way to make sense of life. We need to get back inside. Your family needs you," Ethan said.

"I know they do. Joann needed to hold Tess for a while," Gideon said and turned around and started walking.

The children remained sitting subdued on the steps, but Sarah had returned indoors and sat at the table with Doc and Abby. Joann's wailing had stopped, but she remained in the rocker holding the baby and Zack sat beside her.

"I can't get Tess away from her. I'm not sure she even hears me and Zack just sits there," Abby said quietly.

Gideon walked in front of the rocker and put his hands on its arms to stop the rocking. He reached up and gently grasped Joann's chin and turned her so that they looked eye to eye. In a soft, but firm voice, Gideon said, "Joann, you need to listen to me. You need to let me have Tess and you and Zack need to go rest. You're exhausted. We will talk when you get up."

Joann reflexively held the baby out to Gideon. He took the baby, cradling Tess in his arms. Doc walked over and grabbed his bag. The doctor pulled out a bottle of laudanum and administered two teaspoons to Joann as if dealing with a child. She made a face as she swallowed the medicine, but never spoke. Doc did the same for Zack. Abby came over and took Joann by the hand, leading her to the bedroom with Zack following like a puppy.

Abby returned as Gideon laid the body into the bassinet. The sight of her husband gently tucking the baby in as if Tess were sleeping, crumbled Abby's last wall of stoicism and she collapsed into a chair. Her crying came so hard that she had trouble catching her breath and moments past before she realized that Gideon and Sarah stood on either side of her clutching her shoulders. Neither spoke, but waited for her to cry herself out.

Standing, Abby wiped her eyes and took a deep breath. Her posture slowly straightened until she stood gun barrel straight and she pulled her shoulders back almost unperceptively. "Gideon, we're going to have to hold their hands through this and be the strong ones. Zack might be strong enough, but Joann has never dealt with anything close to this," she said.

Chapter 20

Digging the hole in the ground for the grave seemed to Ethan to be the hardest job he'd ever attempted. He and Finnie took turns laboring at the work. Tess would be buried beside Gideon's mother in the family plot and Ethan had shouldered most of the responsibilities for making all the necessary arrangements. Zack currently seemed incapable of making any decisions. Gideon had his hands full taking care of his family and was in a dark place himself that worried Ethan. Trying to decide where to bury the baby turned into an ordeal of indecision until Ethan had stepped everyone through the idea of burying her beside Martha Johann. He had no desire to be involved with the choice, but nobody else seemed to be functioning well enough to come to a decision.

"Mary's miscarriage was a sad enough affair, but the pain of loving a baby for two weeks before she is snatched from your hands is just unfathomable," Finnie said as he moved to relieve Ethan at digging the hole.

"That it is. I'm worried about all of them. I only hope that time will heal their pain, but I fear it will be a good long time," Ethan said, climbing out of the hole and mopping his brow with his sleeve.

Ethan and Finnie finished digging the grave and walked inside Gideon's empty cabin to clean up. The family had been gone all day to the wake at Zack and Joann's cabin. Rushing to change clothes, the two men felt obligated to hurry back to the wake to help greet neighbors and friends as well as comfort the family.

Upon arriving at the Barlow cabin, both men scanned the yard, surprised by the number of wagons and horses. Word of the baby's death had spread quickly to Ethan's congregation and from there to the town.

"That's quite a showing," Finnie remarked.

"Yes, it is. I'm afraid that it might be a little overwhelming considering the circumstance," Ethan noted.

"Let's go see if we can do our part. Maybe we can help clear them out," Finnie said.

"I probably shouldn't say this, but I dread seeing that poor little baby in her coffin. It's about the saddest thing I've ever seen in my life," Ethan said as he climbed down from his horse.

"I know. It makes me worry about Mary and our baby. I wish she could be here, but Doc wouldn't have any part of it and I don't suppose seeing Mary pregnant right now would do Joann any good," Finnie said as they walked up the stairs to the porch.

The crowd inside the new cabin made maneuvering around the rooms difficult. Food brought by the visitors sat everywhere. Gideon and Zack stood on either side of the coffin greeting people. Joann sat in her rocker with Abby standing by her side holding Chance. The grieving young mother managed to thank people for coming, but made no other attempts at conversation.

Ethan sidled up beside Gideon and forced himself to look down at Tess. Gideon had asked the cabinetmaker to build a beautiful coffin out of the craftsman's stock of walnut. The baby's body rested on a quilt that Abby had made for Tess before her birth and by Tess's side was tucked a ragdoll. Ethan found himself trying to pretend that Tess lay there sleeping. He quickly turned his head away and looked at Gideon.

"How are you holding up?" Ethan asked.

"This is the easy part. Talking keeps me from thinking too much. It's the quiet times that are hard," Gideon said.

"How are Joann and Abby doing?" Ethan inquired.

"Abby is holding up pretty well. I think she may be dealing with this better than I am. Joann is really struggling. I'm not sure she'll ever be the same and it breaks my heart. That girl is too full of life to let the light go out. I just don't know," Gideon said quietly so Zack couldn't hear.

The crowd eventually thinned out until only Ethan and Gideon's families remained. Tired from all the standing, the adults dropped into chairs while the children headed outside to play. Having talked all day, the conversations now lagged and caused an uncomfortable silence.

Seeing the need to take charge, Sarah stood. "I don't know about anybody else, but I'm starving and there's enough food here to feed an army. Everybody needs to eat," she announced.

∞

All of the pews were packed with people at Ethan's church for the funeral. Ethan scanned the room from the podium wishing that he could get this kind of attendance for his Sunday service. Eyeing Tess's family, he tried to determine their state of mind. Joann looked like glass ready to drop on rock. Abby seemed to be coping the best of the bunch. Zack had the appearance of being in a stupor and Ethan doubted that the young man had really yet begun to deal with his grief. Knowing Gideon the best, Ethan knew that an explosion waited around the corner. The only question was when.

Ethan welcomed everyone and led them in a prayer before beginning the service. "Usually, this is a time to reflect on the life of the one that passed. That's a hard thing to do when your life was as short as Tess's was. I will say that Tess was beautiful and a good baby. She brought immense joy to those that loved her during her short life. None of us that were around her will ever forget her and she will live on in our memories forever. At times like these, the question that many ask is why a merciful God would take a baby so young. I know that we all struggle to find a good answer, but I believe it comes down to faith. Just as we have faith that there is a God, we have to have faith that God has reasons for wanting Tess in Heaven. No matter how much we hurt and grieve, we have to keep faith that we'll all be together someday and then we will understand the ways of the Lord. In the days that come, I ask all of you to pray for Joann, Zack, Gideon, Abby, Winnie, and Chance. You all know that these people mean the world to me and I pray that I can be as much comfort to them as they have been to me in my times of need," Ethan said before reading Psalms 23 and leading in the reciting of the Lord's Prayer.

Gideon and Zack arose to place the lid on the coffin before nailing it shut. As they lifted up the top, Joann bolted from her seat and ran to the casket. She bent over to kiss Tess before draping herself across the box.

"Daddy, please don't do it. Please, I can't let her go. She'll be in the dark," Joann cried out.

Looking at his daughter and then towards Abby, Gideon stood at a loss on what next to do. Abby and Sarah walked up, each gently taking Joann by an arm and helping her off the coffin.

"Joann, we have to bury her now," Abby said in a soothing voice.

Joann gazed into her mother's eyes, but Abby wasn't even sure whether her words had even registered with her daughter. They walked her back to her seat and she sat meekly as Gideon nailed the casket shut.

The pallbearers carried the coffin to the buckboard wagon and the procession headed to Gideon's place for the burial. Gideon kept checking the sky. Clouds had formed and looked as if rain could begin at any minute. He figured the heavens would start pouring at the gravesite for one final insult.

After arriving at the homestead, the coffin was placed beside the hole as everyone crowded inside the wrought iron fence surrounding the family plot. Ethan stood at the head of the grave and waited for the people to get into place.

"Let us pray. Dear God, we ask that the angel's guide Tess Barlow to Heaven and look after her. We ask that in the coming days, weeks, and years that you bring healing to her family and that they take comfort in knowing that they will be reunited with Tess in Heaven again someday. We ask these things in your name. Amen," Ethan prayed.

As the ropes lowered the coffin into the hole, Joann threw herself onto the grass and started pounding the ground with her fists.

"No. No. No. You can't have my baby, God. She's mine and you can't have her. This isn't fair. She never got a chance at life," Joann screamed.

Gideon, fearing that his daughter would break her wrists, scooped Joann around the waist and lifted her off the ground. Joann shifted her weight so that her feet touched the ground and broke free of Gideon's grasp. She spun towards him and began savagely beating his chest.

"Daddy, my baby is gone. Daddy, for God's sake help me, please," she pleaded.

Wrapping his arms around his daughter, Gideon enveloped her in a bear hug. His pain for her seemed unbearable and he locked his knees for fearing of crumbling to the ground with her. He tried to squeeze the hurt away. "I know. I know. I'm here for you. I'll always be here for you," he said as Joann sobbed uncontrollably.

Doc left his family and walked over to Gideon and Joann. He pulled a bottle of laudanum from his coat and handed it to Gideon.

"Get her to take a couple of swigs of this. Just keep the bottle, but make sure that it is used judiciously," Doc said.

Gideon waited until Joann had cried herself out before handing her the bottle. "Doc says to take a couple of sips of this. It'll make you feel better," he said.

Joann took two sips and made a disgusting face as she swallowed. She never spoke, but walked over and hugged Zack.

The crowd said their goodbyes to the family and began walking back to their horses and wagons to leave.

"What now?" Gideon asked Abby.

"We'll go back to Zack and Joann's place. I'm going stay there tonight with Winnie and Chance. You can go home later," Abby answered.

Ethan walked over and pulled Gideon to the side.

"Don't be a stranger. I'll be over to visit some. For God's sake, come to me if you need to talk. Okay?" Ethan said.

Trying to smile, Gideon said, "Yes, sir."

By the time they reached the cabin, Joann sat on the wagon seat half asleep. Zack helped her down and into the cabin. She offered no resistance as he led her to the bedroom.

Gideon motioned Zack outside upon the young man's return from the bedroom. They walked out onto the porch and sat in the swing.

"I feel I've ignored you since all this has happened. I've been busy taking care of everyone else. I want to know how you're doing and let you know I'm here for you," Gideon said.

"You know, Gideon, I don't really know how I'm doing. I've been so worried about Joann that I haven't spent much time thinking about things. I'm kind of numb right now," Zack said.

"I can understand that, but I know that it won't last. Losing Tess will hit you when you're not expecting it. You're bound to do some grieving. Take it from someone that knows and don't try to avoid it. It's like an open wound that festers if you don't. You know I think of you as a son. Just come to me if you need to talk," Gideon said and patted Zack on the leg.

"I will. I think I'll go rest," Zack said as he stood.

Zack held the door for Abby as she walked outside and he went into the cabin. She sat down beside Gideon.

"Are you going to be okay alone?" she asked.

"I will. I could use a little alone time anyway. I haven't had much time to think," he said.

"I know you haven't. There's going to be a lot of hard days ahead. I'm worried about everybody," Abby said.

"What about you?" Gideon asked.

"I'll be okay as long as you, Zack, and Joann are okay. I think as long as I pour my hurting into making sure Joann gets back on her feet, then I'll be fine," she said.

Tears welled up in Gideon's eyes. "You know, I really fell for that little girl - easier than I ever imagined. This is going to hurt for a long, long time and I'm never going to forget that smile," he said.

Abby wiped her eyes and leaned against Gideon. "I know you did. I loved seeing you hold Tess. You looked good with a little girl in your arms," she said.

Rubbing his scar, Gideon took a big breath and blew out slowly. "I don't want to talk about it anymore today," he said.

"Go on home. You can come for us in the wagon tomorrow evening," Abby said.

Gideon gave Abby a hug and kiss before climbing up on the wagon and heading home. The slow monotonous pace made thinking way too easy. His mind raced over all that had happened in the last two days and he worried about each member of the family. By the time that he reached home, his nerves were on edge.

He unhitched the wagon and turned the horses out before walking to his saddle. Rummaging through his saddlebag, he pulled out the whiskey bottle and took a long swig. He threw the saddle onto Buck and rode out. The horse hadn't been ridden for two days and Gideon let him run to his heart's content towards a ridge. Gideon pulled Buck to stop when they reached the top and climbed down. He looked out to the west, watching the sinking sun. Words tried to bubble to the surface and he stood there until they were ready to explode out of him.

"God, did you take Tess to make my family suffer the way I made that poor family suffer back in the war? Is that what this is all about? Weren't all the years of my life that I wasted enough? And I asked for forgiveness with all my heart and turned my life around. Wasn't that enough? I begged you to take me instead of Tess. Surely a merciful God wouldn't take the life of a baby to cause a family to suffer. If my sin is not paid in full, what more do you want? Make me suffer, but please leave my family be. What more do you want?" Gideon shouted towards the sky.

Chapter 21

Waking before light, Gideon got up and dressed. He wasn't sure if sleeping alone or the funeral had caused his poor night of rest, but either way he'd done a lot of tossing and turning. His limbs felt as if they had weights attached to them as he moved sluggishly through the cabin.

Riding into town, he beat Finnie to the jail and had the coffee ready by the time the Irishman walked into the office.

"How are you doing?" Finnie asked as he poured himself a cup.

"I didn't sleep worth a damn and I'm too foggy to think about much of anything yet. Just waiting for the coffee to kick in," Gideon answered.

"You know if there's anything I can do, just holler," Finnie said.

A tired smile crossed Gideon's face. "I know and I appreciate it," he said.

About mid-morning, Marcus Hanson, Carter Mason, Andrew Stallings, and Lewis Wise walked into the jail. All four men were ranchers with big spreads in the area and carried a lot of weight in the community. Gideon leaned back in his chair and rubbed his scar. He had no doubts that the ranchers were upset about something and not merely visiting the jail to offer their condolences.

"Gentlemen, what do I owe this pleasure?" Gideon asked as they surrounded his desk. Finnie had left the jail and Gideon felt a bit overmatched by the ranchers.

Andrew Stallings took a step forward and cleared his throat. "Sheriff, on behalf of the rancher's association, we want to offer our condolences over the loss of your granddaughter," he said in a halting voice.

"Thank you. But that's not why you came here. What's up?" Gideon asked.

"I've had some cattle rustled, and as you know, it's been a problem lately. Us ranchers are growing concerned that you're not doing enough to catch the men responsible. We're here to make our concerns known," Andrew said.

Gideon ran his hand through his mop of hair and let out a sigh. He was exhausted, grieving, and in no mood to put up with a bunch of high and mighty ranchers questioning is competency. "Let me guess – the missing herd hadn't been checked on for a few days," Gideon said with a touch of sarcasm.

"That's true, but that doesn't mean you should just let rustlers run around stealing our cattle willy-nilly," Andrew said.

"When in the hell did you decide that I let rustlers run free? I would think by now that you ranchers would figure out to check your herds once a day. It's not like the rustlers can just make cattle disappear unless of course they have a three day head start at it," Gideon said testily.

"I tried keeping a ranch hand with the herd and it got him killed," Marcus reminded the sheriff.

"I know you did. I wasn't recommending that, but most of you can have someone check a herd once a day. If it's too far of a distance, have a cowboy make camp somewhere in between your herds. And another thing - tell your ranch hands not to be talking about your cattle in the saloon. I still think that's how this is all happening," Gideon said.

"Regardless, we expect you to get this resolved. Come election time you wouldn't want all us ranchers thinking you weren't fit for reelection," Andrew said.

Gideon shut his eyes and rubbed his chin. Every fiber of his being wanted to explode in rage at the rancher and he knew no good would come from the outburst and he didn't have the energy for it anyway. He took a deep breath and exhaled slowly. "Andrew, I think it best that you leave right now," he said.

Andrew and Carter exchanged glances.

"Come on, we've made our point," Carter said.

All of the men walked out of the jail except for Marcus. He sat down on the edge of a chair. "Gideon, I want you to know how sorry I am over the loss of the baby. I never made it out there to see her while she was still alive and I can't tell you how much I regret my tardiness. It's weighed heavily on me the last couple of days," he said.

"I appreciate your thoughts. I know that when Joann gets to feeling better that she'll take comfort in knowing that you were at the funeral," Gideon said.

"Is Joann going to be alright?" Marcus asked.

"I don't know, Marcus. I really don't know. She's taking it mighty hard," Gideon said.

Marcus sat rubbing his forehead and didn't speak for a moment. "Okay. I best be going. And Gideon, I know that you'll catch the rustlers. We haven't been much help to you. You take care," he said as he slowly made his way to the door.

"You take care too," Gideon said as a farewell.

Finnie walked back into the jail a short time later. "John Hamilton and his family are about to leave. Mary already said her goodbyes. I expect we should do the same," he said.

"Yes, we should," Gideon said as he stood and put on his hat. "We've had some more cattle stolen. I know I haven't been any use the last few days, but have you heard anything at the saloon?"

"No, I would've already told you if I had. Cowboys talk all the time. I don't know how I can figure out which one is up to no good," Finnie said as he followed Gideon out the door.

Doc and the family stood at the spot where the stagecoach would be arriving. Gideon noted the dour expressions on their faces. For a family from back east that was thousands of miles from their home and out of their element, and an old doctor that had spent his life alone, nobody seemed thrilled with the parting. Gideon smiled at their apparel. All of them were dressed in clothes bought in Last Stand and suited for the west. Even Kate had taken to wearing dresses more practical for a rancher's wife than that of a banker's.

Gideon and Finnie walked up and Gideon shook John and Henry's hands.

"I hate to see you leaving again. You all look like you belong here," Gideon said to John.

"We have to get back home, but we're going to miss this place. I think I could make a ranch family out of them," John said.

"I'd say so. The way Henry shoots a gun, I'm sure I could find a use for him. I don't know if Last Stand could tolerate another bossy woman like Kate though," Gideon teased.

Kate stepped up and kissed Gideon on the cheek. "I'm so sorry for your loss. I'll be praying for you and your family. I'm glad I got to meet you," she said.

"Thank you, Kate," Gideon said.

Finnie shook hands with the father and son. "We're all going to miss you. You've made our grumpy old doctor almost tolerable these last few weeks. I shudder to think what things will be like now with you gone," he said.

Kate gave Finnie a kiss. "I wish we could have stayed for the birth of your baby. I want a good long letter from you and Mary telling me all about that child. Promise?" she said.

"On my Irish honor," Finnie said and put his hand to his heart.

"Let's let the good doctor have some time alone with his family before they leave," Gideon said and the two men departed.

With the stagecoach due to arrive in minutes, Doc hugged his three grandchildren and told each that he loved them. He had already steeled himself for the moment and quickly swiped the moisture from his eyes with the sleeve of his coat. Looking at the three, he still marveled at the depth of love and affection he felt towards them. His body actually ached thinking about their departure.

"We're going to miss you, Grandpa. I wish we could stay forever," Rose said.

"Me too, dear. Me too," Doc said as he brushed his hand down Rose's cheek.

Kate embraced the old doctor. "Meeting you and seeing Last Stand has exceeded all of my expectations by a good bit. I love you and I think it's time that you bring a young doctor into your practice so that you can get away. I know a place back east that would love to have you visit. You better take care of yourself because I plan on seeing you many more times," she said.

"I should have known that you'd have an opinion on what I need to do," Doc said and chuckled. "I love you too. John chose well. Take care of my family."

The doctor hugged his son as the stagecoach came to a stop.

"Father, I really hope you come for a visit. We're already talking about coming back next year, but we'd love to have you come to Boston. Please stay well. We still have a lot of time to make up," John said.

A smile came to Doc's face as he held John at arm's length and looked at him. "We'll see what happens. Take care. I love you," he said.

The driver hoisted the baggage up top to the shotgun rider and the family climbed into the coach. Doc stood on the sidewalk and gazed through the window trying to memorize each of their faces as the stage pulled out. Rose hung her head out the opening and waved until the stagecoach disappeared out of sight.

Doc remained standing in the same spot well after the stage had gone as if expecting it to turnaround and return. A sense of melancholy washed over him and he didn't fight the feeling. He already missed them terribly and he wondered if he'd live long enough to ever see them again. Grandchildren had turned him into one of those old sappy fools that he had always despised listening to brag about their grandkids. Not wishing to be alone, he started ambling towards the jail.

Chapter 22

The previous night, Mary had retired to their upstairs bedroom and as she lifted her arms to pull off her dress, she suddenly found her undergarments drenched. She quickly changed into her nightgown and went to bed. The contractions had started a couple of days prior, but all of them had been mild. Finnie remained downstairs in the saloon helping Delta close up and Mary did not intend to tell him that her water had broken. She felt sure she had at least another day before going into labor and she didn't want him driving her crazy with worry for her and the baby.

She made it through the morning with the contractions only feeling slightly harder than the night before and had managed to tell Doc's family goodbye without betraying any discomfort. As the lunch crowd drifted into the saloon, she served drinks behind the bar while Delta ran around delivering food. She watched as Finnie, Gideon, and Doc walked through the door. Doc shuffled in slowly, hunched over and looking old and frail as if his family's leaving weighed him down. The sight broke her heart and she realized how badly he missed them.

After they sat down, Mary walked over with a tray of drinks and joined them. "How are my three favorite men in the whole world?" she asked.

Doc attempted a broad smile, but failed to conceal his sadness. "I'm busy keeping these two jug heads in line," he said.

"Well, good luck with that. Are you going to be okay? You need to come have dinner with Finnie and me tonight," she said.

The doctor waved his hand through the air. "I'll be fine. I just need a day or two to get my feet back under me. Their leaving has taken the wind out of my sail - I can't deny that. That's some fine children if I do say so myself," he said, smiling at the bragging he'd always detested in others.

Delta sat plates of roast beef, beans, and sourdough bread in front of the men. Gideon and Finnie attacked the meat, but the doctor picked at his meal.

Stopping in mid-bite, Finnie looked at his wife and asked, "How comes you're not eating with us?"

"I'm not hungry. This baby has me feeling plenty full. Oh...," Mary said as she experienced her first hard contraction. She placed her hand to her stomach and winced.

"Did the baby kick you?" Finnie asked.

Mary looked at her husband, trying to decide whether to fib or tell the truth. She felt guilty for not sharing the excitement and decided she wanted to break the news. "My water broke last night and that was my first hard contraction," she said.

Finnie jumped up, bumping the table and sending beer slopping over the glasses. "You should be in bed. We don't want the baby shooting out on this floor with God knows what these cowboys track in here," he said.

Doc grabbed the Irishman's arm. "Sit down and don't waste any more of my beer. Mary is not ready to give birth yet. I'm telling you right now that if you start acting like a fool I'll give you something that'll knock you out until that baby is walking," he said.

"I knew you'd return to your evil self once John departed," Finnie said with a scowl.

The mention of the baby had colored Gideon's disposition and the change didn't go unnoticed by Mary.

"Gideon, I know this talk of the baby must be hard for you. I'm truly sorry for all you and your family are going through," Mary said.

"Hey, you have no reason to apologize. I was just sitting here worrying that your baby will have an Irish brogue. I don't think I could stand listening to two of them," Gideon said in an attempt to make a joke.

"I feel about as welcome as the French pox in a whorehouse. Everybody mistreats the Irish," Finnie said.

"Considering Mary's current condition, I would argue that point," Gideon said with an impish smile.

"I consider Finnie my charity work for the poor and needy," Mary said as the table erupted into laughter and even Finnie smiled.

By the time the men wolfed down their meals, Mary had two more hard contractions. Finnie scooted around nervously in his chair with each sign of pain.

"Let's get you upstairs and check you over," Doc said after his last bite.

Finnie arose from his seat to accompany the doctor and his wife.

Doc pointed his finger at the Irishman. "You have a job to do in protecting the town and you're not needed right now. I'll send for you when the time comes," he said.

The Irishman seemed to melt back into his seat and looked pained, but never said a word.

Doc left to go get his bag and Mary walked upstairs to the bedroom. She shucked off her clothes before plopping into the bed and covering herself with the sheet. Her years as a whore had permanently removed any modestly that she had once maintained.

The doctor came into the room and pulled his stethoscope from the bag. He listened to her heart and lungs before moving to her belly. The doctor moved the instrument several times and his face took on a scowl. Mary could feel her own heart start racing as she waited.

"Found it. Scared me there for a minute. The baby's heart sounds strong," he said.

"Don't do that to me. There's been enough bad news lately," Mary said.

Checking her dilation, the doctor announced, "You still have a ways to go. You probably could even go back to work, but I'd prefer you to stay in bed and preserve your strength. You'll be needing it," Doc said and smiled at her.

"Do you think we're too hard on Finnie?" Mary asked.

"Goodness, no. That muscle on his shoulder would get as brawny as his arms if we didn't keep him in line. After this baby is born I suspect he'll be insufferable," he said.

"I wish John could move to Last Stand," she said.

"Me too, but that's not possible. He has a banking business to run. I'm surprised he's been able to make two trips out here as it is," he said.

"Go on, Doc. I'll be fine," Mary said.

"Why don't I stop by the restaurant and tell Charlotte to close up shop and come sit with you. The lunch crowd will be gone by now and people can eat at the hotel tonight if they want a meal. She can come get me when your contractions get closer," Doc suggested.

"I like that idea. I'm sure I'll see you later," she said and winked at the doctor.

"Uh, go ahead and put on a nightgown," the doctor said in a stilted voice as he departed.

Doc walked to the restaurant and delivered the message to Charlotte before going to his office and tending to patients. Finnie dropped in to see the doctor on the hour every hour for the rest of the afternoon.

At five o'clock on the nose, Finnie walked in and said, "Don't you think you should be over there with Mary?"

"Good God, I'm going over there right now so I don't have to look at you again. I got a Derringer in my bag and I swear if you stick your head in that bedroom one time, that child of yours will be fatherless," Doc said as he grabbed his bag and marched out the door.

The doctor smiled as he walked down the street to the saloon and wondered aloud what he ever did to amuse himself before Finnie came to town. He entered the Last Chance and went straight to Mary's bedroom, finding Charlotte sitting beside the bed. Beads of sweat covered Mary's forehead and she scrunched up her face in pain.

"How far apart?" Doc asked.

"About five minutes. I was just getting ready to go get you," Charlotte answered.

"Good. Let's have a baby before I have to hurt your husband," Doc said.

"Has he about drove you crazy?" Mary asked as the pain eased.

"Not as bad as I pretended. But it's a good thing I'm a sweet natured doctor," he said, smiling wryly.

"I think I'm getting close. At least, I hope so," Mary said.

The doctor performed another examination before proclaiming, "I think we'll have a baby before too long."

Mary let out a groan and sat upright in bed. "Oh, that felt like the hardest one yet," she said through clenched teeth.

"Charlotte, why don't you go find Finnie and tell him to wait in the saloon and then come back up here in case I need you," the doctor said.

Returning a short time later, Charlotte said, "Finnie's pacing down there like a runaway train about to hop the tracks."

A half-hour passed and Mary's pain increased significantly. She twisted and turned in the bed and occasionally let out a whimper.

Doc checked the progress. "The baby's crowning. I can see the top of the head," he announced.

Mary let out a scream. "Doc, are you sure that baby is going to fit through there? It doesn't feel like it," she cried out.

"Yes, you're doing fine," Doc said patiently.

Charlotte stood. "I'll go get some warm water to clean the baby," she said and disappeared out the door.

By the time Charlotte returned, the baby's head had appeared. Mary let out another scream.

"Come on, Mary. Give me one more good push and we'll be done," Doc encouraged.

Mary screamed and pushed with all her might. The baby shot out into the doctor's waiting hands. Doc grabbed his scissors and deftly cut the cord before holding the newborn by its feet upside down and delivering a smack. The baby screamed to life.

"Mary Ford, you have a beautiful black haired boy," Doc announced.

Dropping back onto the pillow, Mary sucked air and waited for the pain to pass. She opened her eyes just in time to see the doctor hand the baby to Charlotte.

"I wanted a little Finnie," Mary said.

Charlotte wiped the baby off and dried him before presenting the little boy wrapped in a blanket to Mary. Doc grabbed extra pillows to prop Mary up as she got her first good look at her child. She studied his face and smiled.

"He's got my hair and eye color, but I don't know who he looks like. The main thing is that he looks healthy," Mary said as she nuzzled the baby against her neck.

"He looks strong," Doc said.

"He's adorable," Mary cooed.

"Charlotte, please go get the father," Doc instructed.

Finnie dashed up the stairs, sounding like a herd of horses, and burst into the room. He froze at the entrance and gazed at Mary and the baby. Tears welled up in his eyes and he smiled at his wife. "What is it and is it healthy?" he asked.

"You have yourself a son and Doc says he's strong," Mary gushed.

"He's a long thing. He'll be taller than you are by the time he's in knickers. Have you picked out a name?" Doc interjected.

Finnie looked at Mary and smiled. She grinned and nodded her head for him to continue.

"We figured there's a name around here that people use so little that they've forgotten who it belongs to. So in honor of our friend and doctor, we decided to name him Samuel Finnegan Ford," Finnie announced proudly.

The old doctor leaned back in his chair and rubbed his chin. A beaming smile came upon his face and he pulled off his spectacles. "That's about the sweetest thing that anybody has ever done for me. Sometimes I about forget that my name is Samuel. I thank you and I'm truly honored. I guess I'll have to start being nicer to you now," he said as he arose and shook Finnie's hand.

"Finnegan Ford, Samuel wants to meet his daddy," Mary said.

The new father picked up his son as if he were afraid of smashing bread and cradled the child against his chest. He gently touched the baby's chin with his finger. "Mary, I love you. Who would have thought in a million years that you and I would have a baby together?"

Chapter 23

After downing his second cup of coffee, Gideon walked outside to sit on the bench in front of the jail. Striking a match, he puffed on a cigar until he got the stogie burning evenly. Leaning back, he crossed his legs and blew out a plume of smoke. He'd given Finnie the day off so that he could spend it with Mary and Samuel on the baby's first full day of life. Finnie had promised to come get him sometime that day so that he could meet the newborn and Gideon wished Finnie would hurry. He really wasn't in the mood to be by himself and was anxious to see the baby. Whenever left alone, he found he couldn't get Tess off his mind and continuously pondered whether he had brought the child's death upon his family.

Doc stepped out of his office, and seeing Gideon, he shuffled across the street and sat down by the sheriff.

"Have you seen Samuel yet?" Doc asked.

"No, I'm waiting for Finnie to come get me," Gideon answered.

"Can you believe they named that sweet little child after me? Who would have ever thought that sawed-off Irishman would be so thoughtful? He's a far cry from the drunk he was when you brought him to town," Doc said proudly.

"Well, listen to you. First, you get all sentimental about having grandchildren and now you're waxing on about having a baby named after you. I'd named Chance after you if I'd known it would have put me in such high esteem," Gideon teased.

"I know it. Next thing you know, I won't be a crotchety old man anymore," Doc said with a chuckle.

"I doubt it goes that far," Gideon noted.

"Gideon, how are you doing?" Doc asked, turning serious.

The sheriff rubbed his scar and thoughtfully blew out a puff of smoke. "I don't know. I guess not so well when I'm alone. Doc, I can't help but wonder if Tess's dying isn't God's way of punishing my family for my past deeds," Gideon said.

"Nonsense. First off, killing that boy was an accident. And nobody has suffered more for a mistake than you did. Since you've been back in Last Stand, you've more than made up for that. Don't forget that Benjamin would be dead if not for you. No, if God worked that way, I'd want no part of faith," Doc said.

"I sure hope so," Gideon said as he uncrossed his legs and knocked the ash off his cigar.

Finnie came strolling down the sidewalk with a lilt to his step. He looked freshly bathed and barbered and he wore his wedding coat. A walking stick would have completed the appearance of a dandy.

"My, my, would you look at you? I doubt Samuel can appreciate your fashion sense at such a young age," Gideon joked.

"I doubt you can either. Mary is ready to receive you," Finnie said.

"Receive me? Am I going to have to bow?" Gideon teased as he arose from his seat.

"You'll have to get rid of that cigar," Finnie warned.

Gideon turned and grinned at the doctor. He gave Doc a wink and tossed the stogie into the street before walking away with Finnie. As they were about to enter into the Last Chance, Gideon looked down the street towards the livery stable. A man stood outside the business with his pistol pointed at Blackie.

"What in the hell in going on now? Finnie, go back to the jail and get a rifle. I'll go see what this is all about. Hide somewhere and if I touch my hat, shoot him," Gideon ordered.

Making a point to clunk his boots on the boardwalk, Gideon walked to the stable. "What's going on?" he asked, trying to sound congenial.

"This blacksmith sold me a lame horse yesterday and I want my money back. I had to walk this nag all the way back here," the man said.

Gideon recognized the horse as one the mounts from the bank robbery. Blackie had bought all the horses that Gideon had brought back, planning to resale the animals.

"That horse was used in a bank robbery. I chased it halfway across the country and brought it back here and I can assure you that it wasn't a lame animal by a long shot," Gideon said.

"Well, it's lame now," the man protested.

"Why don't you put your gun away and we can settle this without trouble," Gideon said.

"I want my money back and my old horse. Even that piece of shit was better than this thing," the man said.

"What's your name?" Gideon asked.

"Joe," he said.

"Blackie, check over the horse," Gideon said.

The blacksmith walked over to the horse and ran his hand up and down the lame leg. He then picked up the foot and examined the underside. "He's got a pebble lodged in his frog. It's irritated," he said.

"Didn't anybody ever teach you to check a horse's foot?" Gideon asked.

"You're just trying to blame me," Joe said.

Gideon rubbed his scar and let out a sigh. He'd about had enough of this nonsense. Too much had happened lately for him to be in a mood to put up with stupidity. "Put your gun away and we'll get this settled," he demanded.

Blackie stepped away from the animal. "I'll take this horse back and give him another of the robbers' horses. They're all of about the same quality and this one will be fine in a couple of days," Blackie said.

"I don't want any of your horses. I want my money and my old horse back. I don't trust you," the man insisted.

"Joe, I'm not going to tell you again to put that gun away," Gideon warned.

"Do you really think you can draw on me before I pull this trigger," Joe threatened.

"No, but I got a deputy with a Winchester aimed at you that will kill you dead if you shoot me," Gideon said.

Joe looked down the street. "I don't see anybody," he said.

"This is your last warning," Gideon said.

Looking down the street one more time, Joe slowly holstered his gun. Gideon pounced like a mountain lion and caught the unsuspecting man with a right hook to the chin. All the rage bottled up in Gideon came lashing out. He wanted to rip off Joe's head. As the man staggered backwards, Gideon waylaid him with a left that buckled his knees.

"You better never draw your gun in my town again. This isn't some damn cow town where you can just shoot up the place," Gideon yelled.

Gideon moved towards the man to hit him again when he felt himself enveloped in a bear hug that felt like a cocoon.

"Gideon, that's enough. You don't want to kill him," Blackie said.

"Damn it, Blackie, let me go," Gideon shouted as he hopelessly struggled.

"Calm down and I will. This ain't doing my arm any good either," the blacksmith said in an unperturbed voice.

"Okay, I don't want blamed for putting you out of work. I still feel bad that you got shot," Gideon said.

Blackie released the sheriff. All the rage had disappeared into weariness and Gideon felt silly for the outburst. Walking over to the man, he took his revolver and unloaded it. He did the same with Joe's rifle.

"Blackie, would you switch out horses and then get him on his way. Tell him if I see him again that he'll rot in my jail until Christmas," Gideon said.

"I'll do it. Thanks for coming to help," Blackie said.

"No, thank you for keeping me from doing something I'd regret," Gideon said before he walked away.

Finnie met him in front of the saloon. "I try to take a day off and the town goes all to hell," he said.

"Let's go see Sam," Gideon said in resignation.

Mary sat rocking the baby when the two men walked into the room. She looked up, smiling as they entered. "I thought maybe you got lost," she said.

"Business got in the way of pleasure," Gideon said wryly.

"Well, get over here and see my baby," Mary said.

Walking to the rocker, Gideon leaned over and moved the blanket away from the baby's face. A smile came upon Gideon and he gently ran his finger down Sam's nose. "Thank God he doesn't look like his daddy," he said.

"That's a fine thank you for somebody that was ready to kill a man for you a few minutes ago," Finnie said and plopped down on the bed.

Mary looked quizzically at Gideon.

"It's not worth mentioning," he said.

"Do you want to hold Sam?" she asked.

Gideon carefully took Sam from Mary and sat down with the baby next to Finnie. He gently bounced the child and leaned down to inhale the baby smell – the same smell as Tess. The aroma seemed as vivid as a photograph. He could sense the wall inside of him tumbling down no matter how much he tried to fight the feeling. The first sob escaped him loud and embarrassingly. Gideon buried his face into the baby and rocked Sam as he lost control of his emotions. He wasn't sure how long the crying lasted and he became aware of Finnie's arm around him and Mary's hand on the back of his neck. Time had seemed to stand still. Wiping his eyes against his sleeve, he said, "Congratulations. You have a beautiful baby. I can't think of two people in the whole world that deserve this little child more than you two. I mean that from the bottom of my heart."

Chapter 24

The creaking of the rocking chair resonated in such perfect time that a clock could have been synchronized to the sound. Joann provided the motion. If not in bed, she could be found in the chair rocking for hours. She slept very little and refused to take any more laudanum. Zack hadn't worked since the death of Tess and spent his days trying to comfort his wife. She only spoke when necessary and spent the rest of her time mourning in silence. Zack sat at the table and watched Joann rock. Her hair looked stringy and greasy and the darkness under her eyes gave the impression of a life lived hard. The muscles in her face had the slack appearance of a drunk stumbling across a room.

Zack had pushed his grieving aside, having his hands full worrying about his wife. He had the help and support of all the others in their circle of family and friends, but nobody seemed able to help Joann try to carry on with her life. Nothing he or anybody else did seemed to work.

Walking to the rocker and squatting down, Zack said, "Why don't I heat you some water and you can take a bath? It'll make you feel better."

"Maybe later. I just want to rock right now," Joann said.

"Can I get you something to eat?" he asked. Her lack of appetite since the funeral only added to his list of growing concerns.

"Zack, I'm fine, really. You should go work," she said without breaking the rhythm of her rocking.

Standing up, Zack walked to retrieve his hat. He contemplated telling Joann about Mary's baby in hopes of cheering her up, but feared the news would more than likely cause the opposite effect.

"I'm just going outside. I won't be gone long," Zack said before walking outdoors.

Zack walked to the pool made by the stream and sat down on a rock that made for a decent seat. He managed a smile as he thought about all the times that he and Joann had gone skinny-dipping there when working on the homestead. Tess had probably been conceived during one of those frolics. Those days seemed liked a million years ago when he thought about Joann sitting in the rocker now. Water welled up in his eyes and he started to cry. He wasn't sure if the tears were for himself, Joann, or Tess – maybe for everybody. The loss of his daughter and the worrying about Joann had left him feeling old and worn down. He tried to keep Tess out of his mind as much as possible. What good could come from dwelling on her? As Sarah used to say, Joann was a spirited girl, and the sight of her now broke his heart. He knew she needed time to grieve, but the depths of her sadness left him fearing that he'd never get his old Joann back. And he needed that hope right now to get out of bed each day and put one foot in front of the other.

Walking back to the cabin, Zack watched as Abby pulled up on the buckboard with Winnie and Chance. He stopped walking and blew out a big breath of air, relieved to see that help had arrived. Abby climbed down and helped the children off the wagon. She stood there waiting for Zack to walk to her.

"How is she?" Abby asked.

"She's going to wear a hole in the floor from all that rocking. I can't even get her to bathe. Abby, I don't know what I'm going to do," Zack said.

"Stay out here and keep an eye on Winnie and Chance and I'll go take care of her. Don't give up. It'll get better in time. How much time is the question," Abby said.

Zack only shrugged. He looked so helpless that Abby had to hug him. Long ago she'd come to love Zack as a son and his struggles made her want to fix his problems as she would Chance's skinned knee. Zack was a good, brave man and seeing him struggling with what life had thrown his way affected Abby as much as Joann's mourning did.

Abby marched into the cabin to find Joann still rocking. Her daughter looked over at her and slightly nodded her head. Walking in front of the rocker, Abby scrutinized Joann and wished that she possessed some magical power to make all the hurt all go away or that she could fix the problem with a good ass chewing, but resigned herself to the fact that time and patience were the only things that would fix Joann.

"I going to heat some water so you can bathe," Abby declared.

"Maybe later, Abs. I'm fine," Joann said.

"That wasn't a question. It was an order. Your hair looks as if you used it to wipe out a skillet after cooking bacon. I bet you stink too. Cleanliness and grieving don't have anything to do with each other and no daughter of mine is going to be nasty," Abby said before heading to warm some water.

By the time the water had heated, the creaking of the rocker had about gotten on Abby's last nerve. As far as she could tell, Joann hadn't missed a single beat in her motion. Abby walked over and held out her arms as if encouraging a toddler to take its first step. Joann grasped her mother's hands and pulled herself to her feet. Abby unbuttoned the back of Joann's dress and pulled it over her head. Joann finished undressing herself and followed Abby to the tub. She stepped in and sat down meekly as Abby poured water onto her daughter's hair and began scrubbing.

"Abs, I don't want no more babies. Winnie and Chance will have to give you grandchildren," Joann said.

"I see. That'll be a long wait," Abby said.

"I'm thinking of moving back to Wyoming and living with Momma and Poppa. I love Zack and it wouldn't be fair to him to live that kind of life with me, but no man is going to cause me to have another baby," Joann said in a voice that sounded childlike.

Abby paused in her scrubbing and gazed at the back of her daughter's head. "Joann, you're not thinking rationally right now. Just give things some time before you make up your mind about the future," she said.

"I can't bear to write Momma and Poppa, have you?" Joann asked.

"I have. I haven't heard back from them yet," Abby answered.

"I couldn't ever replace Tess. That's what another baby would be and it might die too. I had a perfect baby and I don't need another one," Joann said just before Abby rinsed out the soap.

Satisfied that she had the suds out, Abby began scrubbing Joann's hair again. "You're entitled to do all the grieving that you need to do. That's only natural, but mourning and wasting your life away in that rocker are not the same thing. Life has got to go on and you need to start doing your part. Zack is entitled to a warm meal and clean clothes. It's not right to expect him to do everything. He's suffering just like you are. Grieve for Tess. Grieve for your and Zack's loss, but don't stop living. Everybody is here for you, but we can't do it all. You have to help yourself."

Joann did not speak, but her shoulders began to tremble and then she sobbed. Abby didn't say anything. She finished washing Joann's hair and rinsed it again.

"Okay, your hair is finished. Now I want you to scrub that body clean. I'll go find you some clothes and then I want you to go outside and spend some time with Winnie and Chance. You're their big sister and they need to see you act like one. Winnie has been worried to death about you and she needs to see that you are okay. Sometimes we have to pretend for the younger ones. Okay?" Abby said.

Joann nodded her head as she soaped her rag. After she finished bathing, she toweled off and put on the clothes that Abby had picked out. Walking to the bedroom, she emerged with her hair combed. She didn't say anything, but seemed content to follow her mother's orders.

As she headed towards the door, Abby said, "Send Zack in here. I'm going to cook that boy a meal. He looks about half-starved to me."

By the time that Zack walked into the cabin, Abby was heating a skillet.

"I'm making you a breakfast even if it's the afternoon. You look like you could use some bacon and eggs to me," she said.

"That does sound good. I see you got her cleaned up," Zack said.

"I did. I think she might do a little better with taking orders right now than asking her to do something. It'll give you a chance to be the bossy one in this marriage for a change," Abby said, trying to sound lighthearted.

"Abby, do you think she's going to be alright? Will I ever get my old Joann back?" he asked.

"You've got a long road in front of you, but just be patient. You need to think of yourself too and grieve for your loss. If you don't now, it'll surely come back to bite you later. Joann did listen to what I said and I believe it helped. I just think she's going to have to hear the sermon a few times before she becomes a true believer," Abby said and gave her son-in-law a maternal smile.

Chapter 25

Noise from the booming business of a Friday night in the Last Chance Saloon drifted up into the bedroom. Sam slept peacefully in his bassinet, oblivious to the sounds coming from below him. Finnie staggered upstairs early, tired and ready to call it a night. The baby had kept Mary and him up the previous night. Mary had been able to nap with the baby during the day and she was now well rested and itching to get out of the bedroom for a while.

"Finnie, get you some sleep. I'm going downstairs to help out. They're shorthanded and from the sound of things, I'm sure they could use me to pour some beers," Mary said.

"Are you sure you're up to being on your feet that much?" Finnie asked as he sprawled out on the bed.

"I feel fine. A beer mug isn't nearly as heavy as Sam and I've been cooped up in this room for too long," she answered.

"Okay, then," Finnie said in a voice that sounded half-asleep already.

"If Sam starts crying, come and get me," Mary said as she studied herself in the mirror and pinned up her hair.

Walking down the stairs, Mary scanned the room with the practiced eye of a well-seasoned businesswoman. Even for a Friday night, the place looked busier than usual. She walked behind the bar and said, "Who needs a drink?"

Many of the cowboys congratulated Mary on the baby and offered to buy her a drink, which she declined. From across the room she locked eyes with Kurt Tanner. The cowboy smiled and made a salute with his beer mug before he walked to the bar. His step had a slight stagger as he moved. Mary had never seen the young man drink more than a few beers, but that obviously wasn't the case this night.

"Well, look at you. You had your baby and you're already looking as lovely as a schoolgirl. Congratulations. I hear you had a boy. Can I buy you a drink?" Kurt said with a nearly undetectable slur.

"Thank you, but I'm not drinking," Mary said, noticing that Kurt was drunk enough to stare boldly at her breast.

"I'll have me a beer, if you please," he said and winked at her.

Fetching the beer, Mary placed it in front of Kurt. The cowboy reached into his pocket to retrieve his money and raised his hand above the bar as he picked through the coins. Mary spied four Double Eagles, two Eagles, some other coins, and a gold ring. Kurt fished out the two bits to pay her and flashed his patented smile that he thought charmed the ladies.

"Enjoy," Mary said.

"I always enjoy your beer and your company. I'd have courted you if I'd gotten to this town sooner," Kurt said, his inhibition gone.

"That's the story of my life – a day late and a dollar short," Mary said before another patron called out for a beer and she used the request for an excuse to get away.

Finnie never came for Mary and she worked until the crowd thinned considerably. She got the attention of

Delta and the other bartender and said, "I need to go check on Sam. Good job tonight."

"Give that sweet baby a kiss for me," Delta said as Mary started up the stairs.

The sound of Finnie snoring echoed down the hall and as Mary entered their bedroom he never stirred. Sam slept also, but restlessly. Mary picked him up and offered Sam a breast. The child greedily suckled, making her smile. She'd already teased Finnie that Sam liked her tits even better than he did. Sam nursed until he fell asleep. Mary gently put him in the bassinet, changed into her nightgown, and crawled into bed next to Finnie. She stared into the dark hoping that she could go to sleep. Tomorrow looked to be a big day.

In the morning, Mary insisted that she and Sam accompany Finnie to the jail. Finnie eyed his wife suspiciously as she darted around the room getting ready.

"Are you sure we should take Sam out?" Finnie asked.

"Of course we can take him out. He can't stay in here forever. A little sunlight would do him some good. Besides, I'm supposed to bring him to see Doc today anyways," Mary said.

"Why all the interest in going with me to the jail?" he asked.

"I figured something out last night and I need to tell Gideon," she said.

"You know I'm quite capable of repeating to Gideon what you know," Finnie said with a touch of dismay.

"I found it out and I want to tell it. And besides, it'll give Gideon the chance to go ahead and tell me that he told me so," Mary said.

Finnie looked at his wife quizzically, but didn't say anything more. They hadn't been married that long of a time, but long enough for him to know when his situation was futile.

The family walked to the jail and entered.

"About time you got here," Gideon said before looking up from his desk to see Mary and the baby.

"The boss has some big news that she won't share with me," Finnie said defensively as he and Mary took a seat.

With his curiosity aroused, Gideon looked attentively at Mary, waiting for her to speak.

"The saloon had a booming business last night and I went down to help after Sam went to sleep. Kurt Tanner came up to flirt as he always does. First time I'd seen him a little drunk. He went to pay me for a beer and pulled out over a hundred dollars and Colin's gold rope ring," Mary said and paused to let the news sink in.

Gideon leaned back in his chair, habitually rubbing his scar and blowing up his cheeks as he exhaled. "I always thought there had to be a third person in on killing that old sheepherder. What kind of fool would carry the ring around with him?" he mused.

"I never claimed Kurt was the smartest cowboy I ever met. Maybe he just liked it and wanted to keep for himself and he was drunk enough last night to get careless," Mary answered.

"Didn't I tell you about him? I thought something just wasn't quite right about Kurt from the get go. He always struck me as shady," Gideon said.

Mary turned to Finnie and smiled. "I told you that he'd gloat," she said.

Making a sarcastic face, Gideon mused, "I wonder if that was Colin's money too."

"Personally, I never bought into Colin having money. Seemed to me to be something that old men playing checkers made up to have a conversation," Mary said.

"Kurt Tanner is one of our rustlers," Finnie said.

"That's what I was about to say," Gideon added as he looked at his deputy.

"I knew if I led you boys to water that you'd be smart enough to drink. I'd bet my bottom dollar that Danny and Lacey are his accomplices," Mary said, smiling wryly as she spoke.

"I still haven't heard you admit that you actually misjudged a man. You always take such pride in your abilities to size us all up and make sure that we know about it," Gideon chided.

"You're an ungrateful man if I ever saw one. The ranchers are about ready to riot and I came here to help. You're more concerned with me admitting to a mistake instead. Yes, Gideon Johann, I was wrong about Kurt Tanner. I thought he just needed a little nurturing," Mary said in a tone that failed to match her chastising words.

Gideon leaned back and smiled. "That there was better than solving the crime. I love to hear a woman admit that she was wrong. Especially you," he teased.

"You didn't solve the crime, I did. And it's been said many times before, but bears repeating - Gideon Johann, you are a smug man," Mary said, failing to conceal a smile.

Feeling left out, Finnie said, "Would you like me to leave so you two could have a little private time?"

"No, sir. She's your problem, not mine," Gideon said.

"I'm taking Sam to see Doc. You two can take it from here, I'm sure," Mary said as she arose from her seat.

"Mary, thank you. I don't know what I'd do without you," Gideon said.

Mary stopped and smiled. "I wouldn't have this baby if you hadn't brought that little, lovable Irishman sitting there to town. Sounds like a pretty fair trade to me," she said and walked out.

"So do we go arrest him?" Finnie asked to change the subject with the hope that Gideon didn't see how embarrassed he felt over Mary's affection.

Gideon could see the color come to Finnie's face, but decided not to tease him any further. "No, I don't want him to get off with only possessing stolen property. We're going to catch him rustling and get the rest of his gang too. Maybe we'll get to arrest that detective and clerk in Alamosa also. That would make my day," he said.

"So we're going to take turns spending our nights watching his place, aren't we?" Finnie asked.

"Unfortunately. When one of us sees them stealing cattle, we can go get the other one. We know where they're headed and it's not like they can move a herd that fast," Gideon said.

Finnie sighed and his shoulders slumped. "Sounds like the waste of a good bed to me," he said.

∞

Mary carried the baby across the street and into the doctor's office. The doctor sat at his desk reading the newspaper and drinking a cup of coffee. He peered over his spectacles and smiled.

"Good morning, Mary. I wasn't expecting you this early," Doc said.

"I couldn't pass up seeing my favorite doctor as soon as possible," Mary teased.

"I'm going to believe I'd be your favorite even if this town had more doctors than me. Bring Samuel over to the table," he said.

Placing the baby on the examination table, Mary unwrapped the blanket engulfing Sam and stepped aside for the doctor. Doc grabbed his stethoscope and rubbed the chest piece against his palm until it warmed. He then placed it on Sam's chest and began to listen. The doctor moved all around the chest and stomach until satisfied with his work.

"His heart and lungs sound great. He has good color too," Doc said.

The doctor examined the baby's mouth and ears. "He's fit as a fiddle and such a good boy. He never even made a face," he announced.

"Is that it?" Mary asked.

"Well, there's something I wanted to talk to you about," he said.

"Oh," Mary said, concerned with the tone of the doctor's voice.

"Kate mentioned that she thought that I should bring in a young doctor and start cutting back on my work. I've been thinking about it and I kind of like the idea. I tell you, Mary, those grandkids have changed me. I want more time with them before I'm too old to enjoy them. I wanted to get your opinion on the matter," Doc said.

Mary pulled her head back and looked at the doctor in surprise. "Why are you asking me?" she inquired.

"Because I value your opinion. I might ask Sarah or Abby too, but I wanted yours for sure," he said.

"Well, if you can afford to bring in somebody else, I'd say do it. You've earned the right to slow down," Mary said as she wrapped Sam back in his blanket.

"You know me. I've still got the first dollar I ever made in Last Stand," Doc joked.

Chuckling, Mary said, "I don't doubt that. You've never wasted a dime in the Last Chance."

"You know, since I've been around John and his family, I wonder if I've wasted my whole life by never marrying and having more children," he said.

"Doc, if it weren't for you, Gideon, Ethan, Zack, and I would all be dead. Believe me, we don't think that counts as a wasted life," Mary said.

"I suppose you're right. I think I just might start looking to find somebody to bring into the practice," Doc said.

"Well, just remember one thing if you hire somebody – Mary Ford gets to see her favorite doctor when she needs one," she said and leaned over and kissed Doc on the cheek.

Chapter 26

Riding towards Ethan's place after work, Gideon let himself melt into the saddle. He felt his best since Tess had died. For that one day, he refused to allow himself to dwell on his granddaughter or Joann. He just wanted to pretend that everything seemed fine in his little world. The belief that the rustling would soon be coming to an end made the ride feel as if one of those mountains in his view had just slipped off his shoulders.

With the doors to the barn open at each end to aid airflow, Gideon spied Ethan and Benjamin working in its hallway as he rode into the yard. They hustled from stall to stall getting the horses fed before Sarah called them to supper.

"You boys must be starving. I've never known either one of you to work at such a fevered pitch," Gideon called out.

The father and son ignored Gideon until they completed their tasks and walked out into the yard.

"Ranching isn't like sheriffing. We can't put off feeding horses until tomorrow like you can catching rustlers," Ethan chided.

Gideon pulled his head back in surprise and blinked. "Wow, you're playing rough today," he said as he climbed down from Buck.

"Yeah, that was. It hasn't been a great day. Kurt showed up late and was about useless. First time on both counts," Ethan said.

"We need to talk," Gideon said and made eyes towards Benjamin.

Sarah walked out onto the porch to call her family to supper. "Gideon, I didn't know that you were here. I went to visit Joann today," she said.

"How is she doing?" Gideon asked.

"Not so good. Zack has his hands full and I don't have any answers. I know how I felt with my miscarriages and losing Tess is certainly worse, but the thing that concerns me is that she's not even functioning. She needs to get up and do some chores to get her mind off things once in a while to start to heal," Sarah said.

"I agree. I'm going to give her a little more time before I try talking with her. I don't think Zack can get her up and moving," Gideon said.

"What brings you here?" Sarah asked.

"Benjamin, go in and wash up. Your momma and I will be in shortly," Ethan said.

Gideon waited until Benjamin disappeared into the cabin. "I believe Kurt was involved in the murder of Colin Young and probably Reese Calhoun. Finnie and I are going to keep an eye on him to try to catch him rustling again. I need to catch him in the act. Anyways, I don't think you're in any danger, but that you should know all the same. Working for you provides him cover for his thievery," he said.

Sarah folded her arms and raised her chin. "That's terrible. I don't cherish the idea of having a murderer working for us. I thought I could make something out of him and would have never guessed in a million years that he was capable of anything evil," she said.

"Was he rustling last night?" Ethan asked.

"No, he got drunk in the Last Chance and pulled out Colin's ring. I don't have any proof of the rustling. Just putting two and two together," Gideon said.

"I can't pick a ranch hand to save my life. Zack's the only decent one I've ever hired and he fell into my lap," Ethan said dejectedly.

"Aren't you going to gloat that you were right and I was wrong about Kurt?" Sarah asked Ethan.

Smiling, Ethan said, "Hearing you say that you were wrong is reward enough."

"If it's any consolation, there are days that I think that I was wrong about lots of things," Sarah said, giving Ethan the evil eye.

"I'd love to stick around and listen to you two jaw at each other, but I got to get home and eat before I go back out. Just keep an eye on him," Gideon said.

"Are you sure we're safe?" Sarah asked.

"I think so. Ethan keeps too close of an eye on his herd to steal his cattle and Kurt has no reason to harm you," Gideon answered.

"Gideon, be careful and make sure you go see Joann," Sarah said.

"Don't you worry, I will," Gideon said as he mounted the horse.

After riding home and telling Abby of his plans, Gideon found dinner to be an unhappy affair. Abby made no attempt to hide her disappointment that Gideon would be gone every other night for God knew how long and reminded him about how often he'd been absent from his family lately. Concerns over Joann were also taking a toll on his wife. She did give him a kiss and squeezed his ass on the way out the door. As he climbed onto his horse, he wondered if her actions were out of desire for him or just a reminder of what he could be missing out on.

From the porch, Abby smiled wickedly and said, "That'll give you something to think about while you pass the time sitting in the woods. Otherwise, you just might forget what waits in your bed."

"I just might make you do without," Gideon said and winked.

Abby giggled and slapped her thighs. "Be careful my delusional husband," she said.

Gideon rode towards the house that Ethan provided for Kurt Tanner to live in. The cabin sat in a small valley, surrounded by pine covered hills. The knoll to the north gave Gideon a good view of the house without fear of being spotted or heard. Maneuvering his horse through the trees, he tied Buck up and fetched his spyglass from the saddlebag. After searching out a spot with plenty of pine needles for a cushion, he sat down to view the house. Dusk had begun to settle over the land, but enough light remained for Gideon to see Kurt standing in the yard splitting some kindling. The young man gathered up an arm full of the wood and walked into the cabin. A short time later, smoke drifted into the air from the cooking stovepipe.

While passing the time swatting at mosquitoes, the thought occurred to Gideon that Kurt often visited the Last Chance in the evening. Following the young man to town would be necessary to know for sure of his destination. The potential also existed for Kurt to meet his accomplices at the saloon and leave from there to rustle cattle. The more Gideon thought about his plan to capture the rustlers the more his spirit sagged. He feared an arrest could be a good while in coming and involve many a night with little sleep.

Kurt never left the cabin that evening, and around midnight, Gideon came to the conclusion that no rustling would take place that night. He wearily climbed up on Buck and rode home to get whatever sleep he could before morning made its unwelcome appearance.

For the next week, Gideon and Finnie took turns watching Kurt. Both men had followed him to the Last Chance on one occasion, having to hide their horses on a side street. Finnie had been able to take his normal spot in the saloon until the suspect departed, but Gideon, fearing raising suspicion, had sat in the back room and waited for Finnie to come tell him that Kurt was leaving. Each time, Kurt returned straight to his cabin.

Both Gideon and Finnie were getting irritable and bug bitten. Lack of sleep had led to taking naps on the cot in the jail. Abby and Mary were not pleased with the arrangement either and both voiced their displeasure.

Leaving the jail early, Gideon rode home and made a point to play with Winnie and Chance before supper. They played hide-and-seek for a half-hour even though Chance still hadn't quite mastered the concept of staying hidden. Abby managed to take time out from the cooking to come outside to help her son. The family ended the games with a race back to the cabin that Winnie won.

At the dinner table, Abby asked, "How much longer do you think this is going to go on?"

Gideon shrugged his shoulders. "I don't know, but I would hope it comes to an end soon. No cattle have been rustled in a while. I would think they'd about be due to strike," he said.

"Mary and I have decided that if this nonsense doesn't end shortly that we're going to move in together and let you two have each other," Abby said.

"Are you going to leave Gideon like you did Daddy?" Winnie asked.

Abby observed the furrowed brow and pinched mouth on her daughter's face, and realized that she should have known better to say such a thing. "No. No. No. I was only teasing. Gideon is stuck with me for life. Quit your worrying," she said.

Winnie seemed placated and resumed eating her meal without further questions.

After the meal, Gideon departed to his usual spot to watch the cabin. As he sat down on the ground, he shifted his weight from one ass cheek to the other trying to get comfortable. He was still squirming when two men rode up to the cabin. Putting the spyglass up to his eye, Gideon had just enough daylight left to recognize Danny and Lacey, the two ranch hands that freelanced their services. A smile came across Gideon's face knowing that Mary had already informed him of her suspicion that those two would be in on the rustling. Kurt walked out to greet the men before they all retreated into the cabin. Night settled in and as the full moon climbed high enough into the sky to make good light, the three men emerged from the house. They saddled up and headed south.

The light of the moon would make following them easy, but also make getting discovered a problem. Gideon followed at a distance where he only occasional caught sight of the men, tracking more by instinct that anything else. The men continued south and didn't veer to the west towards Last Stand, ruling out a trip to the

Last Chance. The men continued on another few miles as Gideon tried to keep his bearings on where they might be. He believed they were on Hollander Fields' spread, but he couldn't say for sure. Stopping atop a hill with a good view of the valley below him, Gideon watched as the three men came upon a herd of cattle and began driving them east. Judging the size of the herd in the dark proved hard to do, but Gideon guessed that there were well over a hundred head and he begrudgingly admired the men's deftness at working cattle. The men certainly weren't amateurs. Gideon spun his horse around and headed to town.

Finnie had given Gideon a key for just this occasion and the sheriff cursed as he fumbled in the dark to find the keyhole to the back door. After finally striking a match, he let himself into the back room and promptly walked into a chair, cursing under his breath some more. Using matches, he made his way up the backstairs and into the hall. He let a match burn down too far, scorching his fingers and cussing as he dropped it on the floor. Striking another, he made his way to Finnie and Mary's bedroom and knocked lightly. Light appeared from under the door before Finnie opened it. He stood yawning, dressed in a nightshirt and holding an oil lamp.

Gideon chuckled. "Good God, you look like a leprechaun hibernating for the winter," he said.

"What in darnation do you want?" Finnie growled.

"We got them. Let's go," Gideon said.

"You ruined a lovely dream of Ireland," Finnie said as he turned back into the bedroom. He emerged a few minutes later clothed and ready to go.

"Mary informed me that we better get them or there's going to be a couple of dead lawmen tomorrow morning," Finnie said as he led the way down the stairs using the oil lamp.

"Our wives seem to be getting crotchety in their old age," Gideon remarked.

"They hear you talk about old age and you're going to have a lot worse than crotchety to deal with," Finnie said as they walked to the livery stable.

Blackie didn't take being awakened any better than Finnie had. He lit a lamp and stood by idly as Finnie retrieved his horse and saddled the animal.

"Remind me again why I pay you," Finnie said to the blacksmith.

"You pay me to feed and board your horse. Retrieving and saddling are just a courtesy and I don't feel very courteous at the moment," Blackie said testily before disappearing into his room.

Seeing no need to track the rustlers from the spot the cattle were stolen, Gideon and Finnie took the road out of town going east. They rode for an hour in silence.

"I suppose we ought to head south off the road. We should be getting close to them I would think," Gideon said.

"What's the plan?" Finnie asked.

"I hope we can do this without any gunfire. No need to cause a stampede and let some of the men get away. There should be enough dust and noise that we can ride up on the rear man. I'm going to knock him silly. You can be ready to shoot him if things don't go as planned," Gideon said.

"You're liable to bend the barrel on some of these hardheads we deal with. You use your gun more for a club than shooting these days," Finnie remarked.

"I wish that were true. I just don't want to let them get away or us shot," Gideon said as they turned their horses off the road towards the south.

They rode about a quarter of a mile until they spotted the tracks of the herd in the bright moonlight. Following the herd, they turned back east. A half-hour later, they could taste the dust and hear an occasional bellow from a cow. The dust started making it hard to breathe and forced them to pull their kerchiefs over their noses. The silhouette of the rear man came into their view. Finnie drew his revolver and Gideon pulled his Winchester from its scabbard. The sheriff approached from the rustler's left rear and the deputy from the right. Gideon grasped the barrel like a club and coiled the rifle over his shoulder. The rustler heard the horse hoofs at the last moment, turning to see the rifle crash into his head. He collapsed onto the horse's neck as Finnie grabbed the rustler's mount by the bridle. Gideon pushed the unconscious man out of the saddle, sending the rustler to the ground with a thump. Looking all around, neither of the other two outlaws could be spotted with the dust and distance in between them and the lawmen.

"One down. Let's go to the right," Gideon whispered.

Gideon and Finnie began maneuvering around to the side of the herd. By the time they made it around, the cattle were beginning to loiter about from the lack of a push from the rear. Through the dust, they could see the rustler. He had his horse turned sideways looking out over the herd. The rustler spotted the lawmen at about the same time as they saw him. Gideon spurred Buck hard, heading straight at the outlaw. Futilely fumbling for his gun, the rustler watched helplessly as Buck crashed into his leg and the ribs of his mount. The horse's feet lifted off the ground and the animal rolled in midair, its hoofs slashing wildly towards the sky. Rider and horse crashed violently to the ground. Neither made an attempt to get up off the ground. The man's body lay partially under the horse, contorted in a pose that suggested survival an impossibility. A couple of reflexive kicks flailed from the horse's rear legs before the animal grew as still as its rider.

"Danny? Lacey? What the hell is going on?" Kurt bellowed from across the herd.

Motioning with hands for Finnie to continue riding the herd's right side, Gideon put Buck into a lope in hopes of getting behind the herd and getting the cattle moving before Kurt realized what had happened. As Gideon reached the rear, he saw Kurt sitting on his horse staring down at the still unconscious man on the ground. Kurt saw the sheriff and spun his horse around, galloping north towards the road. Gideon spurred Buck into pursuit. The rustler made no attempt to fire upon Gideon, seemingly content to try to outrun the sheriff. Having no desire to shoot Kurt in the back without provocation, Gideon nonetheless did not intend to let the outlaw escape. Gideon despised shooting a horse out from under a rider, but the rustling had gone on long enough and would end that night if he had his way. He brought his Winchester up to his shoulder and with the light of the moon, he drew a bead on the animal's rear. Exhaling lightly as he squeezed the trigger, the roar of the rifle broke the silence of the night. The horse's rear buckled under and the animal dropped onto its front elbows. Kurt Tanner catapulted through the air as if shot from a cannon. Gideon raced towards the prone outlaw, using only his one hand to point the Winchester at Kurt.

"Don't go for your gun or you're a dead man," Gideon yelled.

Kurt rolled onto his back, trying to suck in air to replace the wind knocked out of him. Gideon noticed the outlaw's right arm bent in a grotesque angle that eliminated any chance of the outlaw reaching for his revolver. Jumping off his horse, Gideon moved towards Kurt and snatched his pistol. The outlaw's eyes were watery and rolled up in his head and he struggled to breathe. Gideon grabbed him by his gun belt and lifted his stomach in an attempt to help the outlaw get air back into his lungs.

Finnie came galloping up, having left the herd at the sound of the gunshot. "You okay?" he asked.

"Yeah, I'm fine. Put that horse out of its misery, if you will," Gideon said.

A single shot again ruined the peacefulness of the night. The cattle moved about in an agitated state, but made no attempt to stampede.

"I better go tie up the other one before he comes to his senses," Finnie said.

"Bring his rifle back. We'll smash the stocks out of his and Kurt's to make a splint. His arm is a mess," Gideon said.

Finnie returned shortly with the rifle. He unloaded both weapons and slammed them into the ground until the wooden stocks gave way. Kurt had begun to breathe normally, but he looked to be in shock and didn't speak. As Gideon set the arm, Kurt let out an ear-piercing scream that seemed louder than the gunfire had. Finnie retrieved some leather strips from his saddlebag and began binding the barrels along Kurt's arm as Gideon held the limb in place. The outlaw made a pitiful moan as they tended to him, but offered no resistance. All the fight and flight had been knocked out of him.

"We got one dead and two injured and one horse between them," Finnie remarked.

"We'll have to leave the dead one until morning. How is the other one?" Gideon asked.

"Lacey's coming around, but I think you might have hit him too hard. He's pretty out of it," Finnie said.

"Great. Doesn't sound like they'll be able to ride together. We'll tie Lacey onto his horse and put Kurt on Buck and I'll ride behind him," Gideon said.

"Better you than me," Finnie said.

"Did you check the brand on the cattle?" Gideon asked.

"Yeah, it looked to be a circle around a HF," Finnie answered.

"I thought they were Hollander's herd," Gideon noted.

Getting the two outlaws onto the horses proved challenging. Lacey could barely sit upright on the ground and kept his hands wrapped around his head. Gideon pulled and Finnie pushed to get the outlaw onto his horse. After he mounted, they tied him onto the saddle to make sure he didn't fall off the horse. Kurt acted slightly more alert, but was in considerable pain and shock. He managed to pull himself onto the saddle with a push from Finnie. Gideon climbed aboard the horse and sat behind the saddle cantle with his arms around Kurt like riding with a child.

"Let's go home," Gideon said as he nudged Buck into walking.

They rode back to town at a slow pace, arriving just before five o'clock in the morning. Stopping in front of the doctor's office, Gideon pounded on the door until the doctor groggily appeared.

"I got you some business," Gideon said.

"I don't need business. I need some sleep," Doc grumbled as he eyed the two injured men.

"Doc, I've been up all night. Please be nice," Gideon pleaded.

"Well, get them in here. I should retire and start fishing with Sheriff Fuller. I'm getting too old for this nonsense," Doc said before retreating into the office.

Chapter 27

After Doc finished treating the two outlaws, Gideon locked them into their cells before dropping onto the cot. He felt as exhausted as he had in his days of fighting in the war and his limbs seemed so heavy that he doubted that he'd ever be able to get off the bed again. Sleep came before a single other thought crossed his mind.

Two hours later, Finnie gently tried to rouse Gideon. The sheriff appeared comatose until Finnie called Gideon's name loudly and shook him. Gideon jumped and flailed his arms, smacking the deputy in the chest.

"Damn, you scared me," Gideon said as he tried to clear his mind.

"You nearly made me piss my drawers when you jumped and whopped me," Finnie responded.

The two men looked at each other and laughed.

"We're getting to be like an old married couple. I guess two hours has gone by," Gideon said.

"Yeah, I thought the same thing when Mary woke me. She's in a fine mood that this camping out at night is through for us," Finnie said.

"If you'll go get a buckboard and tarp from Blackie, I'll check on the prisoners. We'll have some breakfast and then get on are way," Gideon said as he climbed off the cot.

The prisoners appeared as tired as Gideon still felt and never stirred when he entered the cell room. He walked out without bothering to awaken them.

Gideon and Finnie each ate a huge breakfast of eggs, bacon, and biscuits washed down with a pot of coffee before climbing onto the wagon to head out to retrieve the body. They arrived at the spot, finding the cattle scattered about rummaging for grass. After extracting the corpse out from under the horse, they wrapped Danny in the tarp and placed him in the back of the wagon along with the tack from the two horses.

They made a stop at Hollander Fields' ranch on their way back. The rancher seemed as irritated that he had to go retrieve his cattle as he was relieved that they weren't stolen. Neither lawman felt especially appreciated for their work as they departed from the ranch.

Once back in town, they left the body with the cabinetmaker and returned the wagon. Both men were fading as they walked back to the jail.

"If you'll make sure those two get supper tonight, I'm going to head home. Get some rest and we'll get a fresh start tomorrow," Gideon said.

Finnie stretched out on the cot. "That I can do. I think I'll nap here. No need getting disturbed by Sam," he said and closed his eyes.

"Sweet dreams, dear. I'll see you in the morning," Gideon teased as he walked outside.

Gideon arrived home to find Abby's mood similar to that of Hollander Fields. She seemed about as upset for having worried and not known where he had been as she was relieved that he returned home safe and sound. After she explained to him the trials and tribulations of being a sheriff's wife, she seemed to notice how tired he looked. He felt too exhausted even to care when she crawled into his lap and began pampering him, but he played along anyways. When she stood up, her spirits seemed lifted and she started cooking an early supper. Gideon's appetite nearly matched his fatigue. He devoured his food, pulling a mouthful of meat off the chicken leg and receiving a reprimand for setting a bad example for the children. When he finished eating, Gideon walked straight to the bedroom and dropped into the bed. He never even realized that Abby joined him later that night.

In the morning, Gideon climbed out of bed feeling like a new man. He had breakfast with the family and stayed around long enough to get the kids worked up into a frenzy with a wrestling match. Winnie giggled continuously as they roughhoused and Chance let out shrill squeals of joy. Before he exited out the door, Gideon gave Abby a kiss and a wink that left no doubt of his intentions for that evening.

"Maybe if you're lucky and a good boy," Abby teased.

"Oh, I feel real lucky. I don't know if I'm a good boy or not, but boy am I good," Gideon responded.

Laughing, Abby pushed him out the door. "I'll be the judge of that," she said.

Riding to the jail, Gideon found Finnie sitting at the sheriff's desk smoking a cigar with his feet up on it. A cloud of low hanging smoke filled the room like a storm front moving through the jail.

"Top of the morning to you," Finnie said, making no attempt to vacate the seat.

"Good morning. You must be feeling good," Gideon said.

"Nothing like a good night's sleep to cure what ails you. Little Sam slept the whole night," Finnie boasted.

"How are our prisoners?" Gideon asked.

"I've already gotten them fed, but they're a sorry looking pair. Both of them are still in considerable pain. I'm sure the good doctor will be over to check on them," Finnie said.

"I'm going to walk over to District Attorney Kile's office and see how he wants to handle this. We're going to have a hard time charging them with anything more than rustling and Kurt for possession of stolen property unless we can get somebody to talk," Gideon said.

"I'll hold down the fort," Finnie said, taking another draw on his cigar and puffing the smoke into the ever-growing cloud.

Gideon found the always impeccably dressed D.A. Kile sitting at his desk making notes on a ledger. The sheriff liked the young district attorney and found him honest to deal with even if the D.A. did wear his future political ambitions on his sleeve a little too boldly for Gideon's liking.

"Sheriff Johann, what brings you here?" Kile asked as he stood and shook Gideon's hand.

The sheriff explained the situation to the district attorney. Kile listened intently and made notes as Gideon talked.

"So you think Kurt Tanner is the ringleader?" Kile asked when Gideon finished talking.

"I do. I don't know that he did the killing, but I would bet on it. I don't think Lacey was even part of killing Colin Young," Gideon said.

"Let's go down to the jail and you can try to rattle them and see what happens. I'd make a deal with Lacey if it meant getting a murder conviction. He'd be smart to keep his mouth shut, but I'll put the fear in him all the same," Kile said as he stood.

The two men walked to the jail finding the door propped open as Finnie aired out the place.

Gideon sauntered into the cell room. "I've talked to the district attorney and you boys are going to be charged with the murders of Colin Young and Reese Calhoun. Sounds like I'll be building a gallows," he boasted.

Lacey took his hands off his head, straightened his neck, and walked to the cell door. "I've never killed anybody in my life. Danny and me weren't even part of killing that sheepherder. That was all Kurt. Both of us wanted to call off stealing that herd the ranch hand was guarding, but Kurt shot him," he said.

"Keep your damn mouth shut," Kurt yelled.

Unlocking the door to Lacey's cell, Gideon said, "You come with me."

Gideon walked the prisoner into the office and shut the door to the cell room. He motioned for Lacey to take a seat and gave a nod to the district attorney.

"Lacey, I'm District Attorney Kile. I'm willing to make a deal with you. In exchange for you telling me what you know and testifying to everything about the rustling and the murders of Colin Young and Reese Calhoun, I'll agree only to charge you with two counts of rustling. You'll probably get five years and be out in three with good behavior. If you chose not to cooperate, I'll do my best to get you two hanged," Kile stated matter-of-factly.

The rustler didn't seem near as concerned about his headache. His face betrayed fear and his hands trembled as he scooted around in his seat trying to get comfortable.

"I'll tell you whatever you want to know. Danny and I didn't have anything to do with killing that sheepherder. Kurt had a couple of friends come through and they helped him with that. Kurt bragged about shooting the old man in the back of the head after they beat him enough to know that there wasn't any money. He kept his ring. On the night that the ranch hand got killed, we spotted him before he saw us. Danny and me wanted to turn around and forget about it, but Kurt snuck up and shot him. I might be a thief, but I didn't want no part in killing somebody. You can't take that back," Lacey said.

"What did you do with the cattle?" Gideon asked.

"We drove them to the Alamosa railyard. The clerk there is Kurt's cousin. He took care of the paperwork for a cut of the money and paid the railroad detective to look the other way," Lacey answered.

Gideon couldn't help but smile as he envisioned arresting those two assholes.

"How many herds did you rustle?" Kile asked.

Lacey thought for a minute and used his fingers to count. "Six counting the one we got caught stealing," he said.

"Do I have your word that you will testify to all this in court?" Kile asked.

"Anything to keep from hanging," Lacey answered.

"If I were you, I wouldn't talk to Kurt from here on out," Gideon said to Lacey before leading him back to his cell.

Gideon walked back and sat down at his desk. He pulled Colin Young's ring from his desk drawer and handed it to the D.A. for safekeeping. "What now?" he asked.

"You had the railroad part all figured out. Go ahead and arrest them and I'll get a subpoena to get the railroad's books. Make me a list of all the dates that cattle were reported stolen. With Lacey's testimony, we can't lose. You two did a fine job. Good day, gentlemen," Kile said as he stood.

Gideon grinned and glanced at Finnie. "We'll arrest those two with pleasure," he said.

After the district attorney had gone, Finnie asked, "Are we going today?"

"Sure. I was sitting here debating whether to take a wagon to Alamosa or bring a couple of extra mounts with us. I think we'll get a couple of horses from Blackie. It'll be quicker and beat riding on a buckboard," Gideon said.

A heat wave had moved into the area and the day had already grown warm by the time Gideon and Finnie departed from Last Stand. Each man had an extra horse tied to a lead rope following behind him. Gideon planned to be home at a decent time and he pushed the pace. The horses worked up a lather and the two men found themselves continuously mopping their brows with their shirtsleeves. They arrived in Alamosa early in the afternoon and tied the horses in front of the jail.

The sheriff of Alamosa sat at his desk filling out paperwork and looked up in surprise when they walked into his jail.

"Sheriff Johann, you're back. That railroad detective about wore me out complaining about you spying on him," the sheriff said.

"Sheriff White, I'm here to arrest him and that clerk. We got them this time. Since this is your town, I thought you should be with us when we make the arrest," Gideon said.

"With pleasure. I never liked that detective anyways. His name is Shores, by the way. He's about as pleasant as a hungry bobcat," the sheriff said as he stood and put on his hat.

The three men rode down to the railyard, tying their horses on the street.

Gideon said, "If you don't mind, I'd like to walk in there first. He threatened me the last time I was here and I want to give him a chance to make good on his promise."

Sheriff White smiled. "Have at it," he said.

Wandering around the railyard, Gideon finally spied the detective. He deliberately walked towards the man until Shores recognized him. The old Confederate began marching towards Gideon as fast as his limp would allow. He pulled out his nightstick as he moved.

"I told your Yankee ass what would happen the next time I saw you here," Shores yelled as he drew near the sheriff.

Gideon stood patiently until the detective was little more than a step away. With an agile move, he kicked the exposed detective in the groin. Shores doubled over in pain and Gideon delivered a windmill punch to Shore's face, sending him sprawling onto his back. With his revolver drawn, Gideon stuck the barrel against Shores' nose.

"You are under arrest for your part in a rustling ring," Gideon snarled and reached down and removed the detective's pistol.

All the bluster had vanished from Shores. He turned his head and spat out blood, but had nothing to say.

Sheriff White and Finnie walked up to the two men.

"Go ahead and get the clerk. Your deputy and I will keep an eye on this one," Sheriff White said.

Gideon walked to where the clerk worked and went inside the building. The clerk had his head down and never bothered to look away from his ledger.

"Excuse me," Gideon said.

The clerk looked up and scowled at the sight of the sheriff. "Shores warned you what would happen if you came back," he said.

Moving like a cat, Gideon advanced towards the clerk. He clenched the clerk's forehead and shoved. The clerk and his chair flew over backwards, crashing to the floor. Gideon had learned long ago that nothing worked better than having a gun shoved in a man's face to make him go meek. He stuck his revolver against the clerk's nose.

"You are under arrest for helping your cousin steal cattle. You can get up peaceful like or I can drag you out of here. Your choice," Gideon said and sneered at the clerk.

"I'll walk. Just don't hurt me," the clerk pleaded.

"What's your name?" Gideon asked with the gun still touching the man's nose.

"Thad Hill," he answered.

"Start walking," Gideon said as he straightened up and holstered his Colt.

Gideon and Thad walked to the other men. Detective Shores still sat on the ground spitting blood.

"Get up. We have to get back to Last Stand," Gideon ordered.

Shores stiffly got to his feet. He still had trouble standing erect and supported his crotch with his hand as he hobbled towards the horses.

"Aren't you going to tie them up?" Sheriff White asked.

"No, I'd rather give them the opportunity to try to escape and then shoot them. Saves having a trial that way," Gideon said and winked at his counterpart.

"Sheriff White, you have a responsibility to escort us back to Last Stand. That man is liable to kill us as soon as we get out of hearing range," Shores pleaded.

"I don't think he will unless you give him a reason. I'd start being more polite if I were you," Sheriff White said.

"Thank you, sheriff," Gideon said and shook the sheriff's hand.

"I'm sure will be crossing paths again," Sheriff White said before mounting up and riding away.

"Let's head home. The last couple of days have been so good that I plan on doing a little celebrating tonight," Gideon said and winked at Finnie.

Chapter 28

Standing out on the front porch, Gideon sipped his coffee as he watched Winnie and Chance running around the yard like a couple of wild Indians. Considering the two children's age difference, he marveled at the amount of time Winnie devoted to her younger brother. She could never be accused of not taking her job of big sister seriously and Gideon felt a burst of pride welling up for the child that had once loathed him.

Relieved that Saturday had finally arrived, Gideon had no intentions of going to town that day. He planned to check the herd and visit Joann. Finnie would see to the prisoners getting fed. Gideon despised housing prisoners and anxiously waited for the trials to begin. He'd met with D.A. Kile again and the confident district attorney had once again assured him that they'd get convictions on all the men. The prosecutor planned to serve the subpoena on the railroad come Monday and the trial would begin on the judge's next scheduled appearance in Last Stand.

Abby walked out onto the porch. She took Gideon's hand, draped his arm over her shoulders, and leaned into him.

"That's a couple of fine looking children if I do say so myself," she said.

"That they are. I guess I can't even say anything bad about Winnie's daddy now that Marcus and I have made peace," Gideon said and smiled down at his wife.

"Please don't. He's actually looked me in the face the last couple of times I've taken Winnie to see him and even acknowledged Chance's existence," Abby said.

A rider came into view coming up the driveway. From the color of the horse and the way the rider sat in the saddle, Gideon recognized the horseman as Zack. His son-in-law rode into the yard and jumped down from his horse, scooping Winnie and Chance up under each arm. He somehow managed to hold and tickle them at the same time until he'd extracted kisses from each child. With his mission accomplished, he released his quarry and walked onto the porch.

Abby remained tucked under Gideon's arm as Zack approached them.

"What brings you out here?" Abby asked.

Zack looked out into the yard to make sure that Winnie wasn't listening. "I don't know what I'm going to do with Joann. She'll be better for a day or two after you or Sarah talk to her and then she slips right back into sitting in that rocking chair all day. Ethan needs help now that Kurt is in jail and I need to do things on our homestead, but I hate leaving her alone that way. She won't listen to me. I'm worried about her and I'm about at my wits' end," he said.

Moving a step away from Gideon so that she could see her husband as she talked, Abby said, "Gideon, maybe you need to go talk to her. Sometimes a girl needs to hear things from her father."

Gideon started rubbing his scar. "I don't know about that. Sarah is the one that's good for a fire and brimstone sermon when one is needed," he said.

"I'm not sure that is what is called for this time. Sarah needed to light a fire to get Mary out of bed after

her miscarriage and to try to get you to straighten out your life, but I don't think that is what Joann will respond to – she needs encouragement. I think she needs to hear from you that she has to get back to being a wife and that time heals," Abby said.

Still unconvinced, Gideon said, "Maybe she needs to hear it from the man that raised her. Your Uncle Jake and Aunt Rita need to get down here."

"Yes, they do and they're planning on coming next month. That's the earliest that they can get away. What's with you? I've never seen you so hesitant to help out on something in my life," Abby questioned.

"I'm just not sure that somebody that wasted fourteen years of their life running from their troubles is the one to be preaching to Joann. And it's not like I've been around that long being a father to her," Gideon said as he dropped into the swing.

"Now you're being silly. That's exactly why you should be the one to talk to her. And that father-daughter thing is nonsense. You know darn well that she thinks of you as her daddy," Abby said.

Zack watched the exchange going back and forth and began feeling hopeless. "Please, Gideon," he pleaded.

Gideon looked at Zack and then towards Abby. "Of course I'll do it. I planned to go see her today anyway, but I just question if I'm the right one to talk to her or if I can even do it. This is still raw to me too. Sometimes I can barely stand to let myself think about Tess," he said.

"I know, honey, but I think she needs her father right now," Abby said.

Abby turned to Zack. "What about you? How are you doing?" she asked.

A pain-laced smile crossed Zack's face and his eyes moistened. "I'll be fine as long as Joann gets better. She needs to get out of that damn rocker and do something. I can hardly think about Tess for worrying about Joann," he said.

Stepping towards Zack, Abby hugged him. "Things will get better. She's too strong not to bounce back," she said.

The thought of confronting Joann made Gideon feel restless and want to pace. He stood up and looked out into the yard. Winnie and Chance chased the dog and Gideon wondered why life couldn't stay as simple as that of a child. Once adulthood came, the other side of every hill seemed to have sorrow waiting there to grab you. He pondered if humans were built so that they required bad times in order to appreciate the joys of life. If true, he questioned if it were really worth the costs. Watching Red run around with the kids, he decided that a well-loved dog might have the best of all worlds.

"Gideon, are you leaving now?" Abby asked.

Forced from his reverie, Gideon turned towards his wife. "I guess I better. I think I'll go in the wagon and take her for a ride," he said.

"I wonder if taking her to see Mary and Sam would do her good or upset her," Abby mused as much to herself as to the others.

"I think that might be a bit too much. What do you think, Zack?" Gideon said.

Zack shrugged his shoulders indecisively. "I don't know. Nothing else is working," he noted.

"I'm going to go hitch the wagon. I'll think about it and play it by ear," Gideon said.

"I'll see you later," Abby said before kissing Gideon goodbye.

Turning to Zack, Gideon said, "Go fishing or go see Ethan. Do something that you enjoy and get your mind off your troubles for a while."

Zack nodded his head.

On the ride over to see Joann, Gideon tried to imagine saying all the things he needed to tell his daughter. Frustrated at his lack of imagination, he gave up on the endeavor. He had no idea what kind of a mood she might be in and their conversation would surely be dictated by that more than what he wanted her to hear anyhow.

As he pulled the wagon into the yard, he found Joann sitting on the steps of the porch. Her hair looked damp from a washing and she wore one of her Sunday dresses. She remained sitting idly as Gideon climbed down from the wagon.

"You look pretty. Are you feeling better?" Gideon asked.

"I don't know. I just needed to feel like somebody again so I took a bath and put on this dress," Joann answered.

Joann stood up and Gideon realized how thin his daughter had become. She appeared to be skinnier than before she became pregnant. Her cheeks were sunken, making her cheekbones jut out, and her large blue eyes look too big for her face.

"How about we ride to town and go to the café. I'll buy you a big steak or biscuits and gravy - anything you want. You need to put some meat on those bones or one of those mountain storms is liable to blow you away," he said.

He could see her mulling over the proposition and she looked unsure whether she liked the idea.

"Okay, let's go," she said as if it were against her better judgement.

On the ride into town, Gideon kept the conversation on any subject but Joann. To kill the silence, he went into great detail about the rustling case and solving the crimes. The closest he came to getting into a problematic topic was mentioning Chance's latest escapades and his expanding vocabulary.

Gideon pulled the wagon in front of the café and helped Joann down. After taking their seats, Charlotte quickly came to take the orders. Both father and daughter ordered steak and potatoes with a side of beans. Charlotte returned with their food a short time later. As they ate their meals, a few people came by the table to say hello and a couple others offered their condolences. Joann seemed unfazed by the interruptions and attacked her food as if she were starving.

Watching his daughter closely to try to judge her state of mind, Gideon debated whether to mention visiting Mary and the baby. The day had gone so well that he was tempted not to bring up the subject, but also feared nothing would be resolved without getting Joann to talk about her feelings.

"I was sitting here thinking that maybe we should stop in and see Mary and Sam. Mary's been asking about you a lot. I know she hated that she didn't get to see Tess or come to the funeral," Gideon said.

Joann's jaw set and she placed her fork on the plate. She looked Gideon directly in the eyes. Gideon had no idea what she might be thinking or what she would say, and he took a bite of steak in an attempt to seem casual.

"Is that why you brought me here?" she asked in an aggressive whisper.

"No, I brought you here because you're too skinny. I just thought we might kill two birds with one stone. I know Mary would like for you to see Sam and she's missed you. She is your friend. You can't hide away in that cabin forever," he said.

Joann continued staring at him as if trying to determine whether he had told the truth. Not wishing to seem guilty, Gideon met her stare head on.

"Daddy, I don't know if I can stand seeing a baby," Joann confessed.

"It's your decision, but holding a baby might do you good. Sam might not be Tess, but a child is a powerful and healing thing to hold in your arms. I can attest to that," Gideon said.

Looking up towards the ceiling, Joann let out a big sigh. "We can try it. I might end up bolting from the room, but we'll see," she said.

Eating the rest of the meal in silence, Joann now ate slowly and the apprehension showed in her face as she meticulously chewed her food. Once finished, Gideon paid for the meal and they walked over to the jail. Finnie sat at the desk cleaning his revolver.

"What brings you to town?" Finnie asked.

"We've come to visit Mary. I was hoping that you could go see if now would be a good time," Gideon said.

Finnie looked at Gideon and then at Joann. "Sure. Sure. I'll be right back," he said as he scrambled from his seat.

Gideon checked on the four prisoners while waiting for Finnie. He had put Shores and Hill in a cell together so that Lacey would not share a share a cell wall with any of the others for fear they might try to kill him. With the arrests in Alamosa, the others had figured out that he had talked and continually harassed and threatened him.

Finnie returned in short order. "Mary says to come on up to the bedroom. She's ready," he announced.

Taking Joann by the arm, Gideon guided his daughter to the alley and through the back door of the saloon. He led her up the stairs to the bedroom and knocked on the door.

"Come on in," Mary called out.

Gideon opened the door and ushered Joann into the room. Sam lay on the couples' bed shaking his arms and kicking his legs. Mary moved catlike to Joann and embraced her.

"I've missed you. I so wanted to see Tess and come to the funeral, but Doc would have none of it. I'm so sorry, Joann," Mary said.

Joann squeezed Mary and buried her face against the other woman. "Thank you," she stammered.

Mary grasped Joann by the shoulders and held her at arm's length. "You're too skinny. You need to start eating. Do you want to hold Sam?" she asked.

Joann looked down at the baby and studied him. "I think so," she said before sitting down on the bed.

Already an expert at handling infants, Joann swooped Sam up into her arms. She looked down at his face before pressing him tightly against her chest. Twisting her torso side to side, she rocked Sam. "He's absolutely beautiful," she said. Her eyes welled with tears and she squeezed her mouth tightly shut as she looked at Mary.

"We think he's pretty special. I have to get after Finnie to leave Sam alone when he's sleeping," Mary said.

Joann bent over and kissed the baby on the forehead. She inhaled his scent with a long breath. "I wish you could have seen Tess. She looked beautiful too. They would have made a pretty pair," she said as her shoulders began quivering and a sob escaped her.

Mary sat down beside Joann and wrapped her arm around the younger woman's shoulders. She leaned in close. "Don't give up. You'll have your time too. I know you miss Tess, but you have to carry on for her and her future brothers and sisters. You're too special not bring life into this world. Okay?"

Joann nodded her head, but didn't reply.

Waiting a few minutes as the women talked about baby stuff, Gideon wondered if his daughter had reached her limit. "We better go," he said.

Passing the baby to Mary, Joann said, "Thank you. I'm glad we stopped in. And give Sam a kiss for me tonight." She jumped up and used her fingers to wipe out her eyes. Turning towards Mary, she forced a smile.

"I'll be coming out to see you soon," Mary said.

Gideon and Joann walked quickly back to the wagon and headed out of town. Neither spoke as they rode. Seeing Joann holding Sam had made Gideon ache for Tess. He had been too busy the last few days to dwell on the loss, but now her death seemed as fresh as the day that they had buried the child. Sitting up straight, he sought to project the strength he wasn't feeling.

"Sam could die tomorrow. Babies are so helpless," Joann blurted out.

Gideon looked over at his daughter. "Yes, he could and so could you or I. Anybody can die. That's life. That's why it's so important to make the most of it. Live everyday like it's your last," he said before turning the horses off the road and heading up a ridge.

The steepness of the hill made the horses strain as they pulled the wagon. Gideon coaxed the animals on by popping the reins until they reached the top. To the north stretched a massive mountain range. Snow still covered the very tops of the gray granite peaks and the valleys looked deep green with the summer grasses. A single eagle floated in the wind as if he ruled all as far as the eye could see. Gideon found the scene awe-inspiring and wished he knew how to paint landscapes. He secretly longed to replicate the beauty of the mountains even as they made him feel small and impotent.

"Maybe I'm not strong enough for life," Joann remarked.

"Nonsense. You're every bit as strong as Abby or Sarah for that matter. You've just been dealt a terrible blow," he said.

"I don't know anymore," she said.

"Joann, look at those mountains. I can feel God in them, and if there's a God, there has to be a plan to all of this. I don't have any of the answers and I don't know why Tess's time on earth was so short or why we're left to deal with her loss. But we all have to carry on with our lives," Gideon said, his voice trailing off.

"But you wasted fourteen years of your life running from your conscience and now you and everybody else act as if I'm supposed to go on and pretend like nothing ever happened," Joann accused.

"That's right, I did waste all that time and that's why I know better than anyone what I'm talking about. They say that time heals. That's a load of horse manure. Time doesn't heal anything. Healing begins when you accept your loss and learn to live with it. Nobody is asking you to get up tomorrow morning and act like Tess had never been born. We're all asking you to get up and start living again. Mourn all that you need, but don't sit in that damn rocking chair all day long being sad. I expect you'll still grieve for Tess on the day you die. I know that I will be. It's okay to laugh again or to go to a dance. Running for fourteen years didn't make that little boy's loss any less tragic and sitting in that chair won't make Tess's loss any more meaningful. Zack deserves better of you and you deserve better of yourself. Don't waste all that time like I did. Begin living again," Gideon said, his voice breaking up until he couldn't speak.

Joann looked at her father. Tears streaked her face and her eyes were red and swollen. Her mouth quivered before she spoke. "I'll try, Daddy. I promise I'll try."

About the Author

Duane Boehm is a musician, songwriter, and author. He lives on a mini-farm with his wife and an assortment of dogs. Having written short stories throughout his lifetime, he shared them with friends and with their encouragement, he has written his fifth novel *Last Ride*. Please feel free to email him at boehmduane@gmail.com or like his Facebook Page www.facebook.com/DuaneBoehmAuthor.

Made in the USA
Lexington, KY
10 September 2016